'**Francesca Marsden.**' His voice sounded husky. Sexy as hell. '**You do realise I'm completely naked?**'

'Mmm.' She couldn't quite get her mouth to move round a proper word.

'And you've just put your arms round me?'

'Uh-h-h.' Someone had glued her tongue to the roof of her mouth.

'And you're in bed with me,' he said softly. 'In *my* bed. Wearing nothing but a very skimpy nightdress.'

She suddenly couldn't breathe.

He grazed his cheek against hers. 'This isn't supposed to be happening.' His breath was warm against her ear, and then he was nuzzling her neck. Tiny, teasing brushes of his lips against her skin. Everywhere he touched became supersensitive, and she wanted more. So much more. She wanted him to touch her everywhere. Kiss her everywhere. Make her forget the misery of seeing the wreck of her flat.

She remembered the way he'd kissed her at the party. The way he'd sung to her. The way she'd wanted to be in his arms, wanted to make love with him.

He dragged in a breath. point of no return. So have to say so right now

She swallowed hard. 'N

D0993881

Bestselling star author of Medical Romance™
and Modern Extra

Kate Hardy

About THE CINDERELLA PROJECT:

'Kate Hardy makes her Modern Extra Romance debut
with a spellbinding romance that sparkles with passion,
sensuality and attitude!…Sexy, sassy and witty…
Kate Hardy's writing simply shines! Readers cannot
help but love her heroine Cyn, who is intelligent,
funny, but who has hang-ups about her body which
women everywhere will relate to, and Max
is a delicious hero you cannot help but adore!'
www.cataromance.com

About STRICTLY LEGAL:

'*Strictly Legal* is Kate Hardy's second title
for the Modern Extra Romance series and it's a
fabulously sassy, sexy and stylish romantic novel
which will be heading straight to your keeper shelf!
Tender romance, sizzling sexual tension, characters
which leap off the pages and master storytelling make
Strictly Legal a compelling modern romance which is
absolutely impossible to resist!'
www.cataromance.com

BREAKFAST AT GIOVANNI'S

BY
KATE HARDY

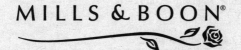

First published in Great Britain 2007
Harlequin Mills & Boon Limited,
Eton House, 18-24 Paradise Road, Richmond, Surrey TW9 1SR

© Kate Hardy 2007

ISBN-13: 978 0 263 85392 6

Set in Times Roman 10½ on 12½ pt
171-0707-57112

Printed and bound in Spain
by Litografia Rosés, S.A., Barcelona

Kate Hardy lives on the outskirts of Norwich with her husband, two small children, a dog—and too many books to count! She wrote her first book at age six, when her parents gave her a typewriter for her birthday. She had the first of a series of sexy romances published at twenty-five, and swapped a job in marketing communications for freelance health journalism when her son was born, so she could spend more time with him. She's wanted to write for Harlequin Mills & Boon since she was twelve—and when she was pregnant with her daughter, her husband pointed out that writing Medical Romances™ would be the perfect way to combine her interest in health issues with her love of good stories. Now Kate has ventured into Modern Extra Romance, and this is her fifth novel for the series.

Kate is always delighted to hear from readers—do drop in to her website at www.katehardy.com

Next month, look out for Kate Hardy's
Medical Romance™ novel
THE ITALIAN GP'S BRIDE

Recent books by the same author:

Medical Romance™
THE CONSULTANT'S NEW-FOUND FAMILY

Modern Extra
IN THE GARDENER'S BED

For Jim—who has taught me much—with love.

CHAPTER ONE

SHE looked as if the world had ended, hunched over an empty coffee cup, staring out of the plate-glass window but not seeing anything.

Gio couldn't leave her sitting there in such obvious misery. So even though he should've locked up ten minutes ago, he did exactly what his father would've done. He made a cappuccino and slid it on to the table in front of her. 'Here,' he said softly.

She looked up, her eyes widening in surprise. 'I...' She'd obviously been about to protest that she hadn't ordered the coffee. But then she smiled ruefully and cupped both hands round the mug, clearly taking comfort from its warmth. 'Thanks.'

'No problem.' He handed her a chocolate dipper. 'You look as if you need this.'

'I do,' she admitted. 'Thanks. I appreciate this.' She rummaged in her handbag for her purse. 'How much do I owe you?'

He waved a dismissive hand. 'Nothing.'

She frowned. 'Won't you get into trouble with your boss?'

'Doubt it.' He smiled. 'Anyway, you're a regular, so call it a refill.'

Those beautiful blue eyes—the same blue as the sky on a

summer evening, he saw, now that he was this close to her—narrowed slightly. 'Regular?'

He shrugged. 'On Wednesday mornings, you order a cappuccino and an almond croissant to go at ten past nine.'

The suspicion on her face morphed into nervousness. 'How do you know that?'

Oh, lord. Obviously she thought he was some kind of weirdo—that he'd been watching her or stalking her. He shouldn't have mentioned the time. 'Work here long enough and you get to know the customers,' he said lightly, hoping it reassured her. 'I'm out of croissants or I would've brought you one—hence the chocolate.' He spread his hands. 'Because that's what women need when things get tough, right? Or so my sisters always tell me.'

'Right. And thank you.' She looked very close to tears.

'Want to talk about it?'

She looked around, as if suddenly realising she was the only customer. 'Oh, lord. Sorry. I'm holding you up.'

'Not at all. Though would you mind if I put up the closed sign and put the bolt on the door, so I don't get a sudden rush and end up staying open a lot later than usual?'

Fran thought about it. He'd actually asked her first, to make sure she didn't feel threatened. And a man who'd brought her a coffee and a chocolate dipper couldn't be all bad, could he? OK, so he knew her Wednesday-morning order—but, as he'd said, you got to know your regulars in business. Just as she did: she recognised voices on the phone and knew even before they asked which ones would be asking for a last-minute panic job and which ones would be booking slots for weeks ahead.

'Sure,' she said.

He bolted the door, turned the sign over to read 'Closed' from the outside, turned off one of the banks of lights, and came to sit opposite her. 'Gio Mazetti,' he said, holding out his hand.

She took it, and was surprised at the sudden tingle in her fingertips when her skin touched his. 'Fran Marsden. And thank you for the coffee, Joe.'

'Gio,' he corrected with a smile.

Now she was listening properly, she heard it. The soft *G*, the *I* and *O* sliding together almost after a pause.

'Short for Giovanni,' he added helpfully.

And then the penny dropped. Of course he wouldn't get into trouble for making her a coffee for no charge. Because the café was called Giovanni's. 'You own the place.'

He lifted one shoulder. 'It's a family concern—but, yeah, I'm in charge.'

'I, um…' She shifted in her seat, embarrassed at her naïvety. 'Sorry.'

He laughed. 'Don't apologise. I'm glad I come across as one of the baristas—there's nothing worse than having the boss supposedly doing a shift and just throwing his weight around instead of doing something useful.'

He had a nice laugh. Good teeth, even and white—no fillings, either, she noticed. A guy who took care of small details. But he also didn't look like the type who went in for cosmetic dentistry. She'd put money on him not going to the gym, either—she had a feeling that Gio Mazetti was in perfect shape from hard work, not from pumping iron. He was good looking, but far from being vain about it.

'So. Want to tell me about it?' When she said nothing, he added softly, 'My *nonna*—my Italian grandmother—always says that a problem shared is a problem halved.'

Homespun wisdom. Just the sort of thing her mother would come out with.

Her mother…

Fran's smile faded before it had had a chance to start. She was going to have to call her parents tonight and admit to them that she was a failure. Not only was she the only one of their children not to get a degree, now she was the only one who didn't have a decent job. And it went right with the territory of not being their real child, anyway—the only one of the four Marsden children who was adopted.

She sighed. 'I lost my job today.'

'I'm sorry. That's tough.'

It wasn't his fault. And he was right—it felt good to unburden herself. Lose some of the sick feeling of failure. 'My boss decided he wanted a new challenge, so he sold the business to go travelling for a year and to work out what he wanted to do with his life.' She shrugged. 'A competitor bought the business. And you really don't need two office managers when you're merging two companies and need to cut your running costs. So one of them has to be made redundant.'

'So you're an office manager?'

'Was.' She pulled a face. 'Ah, ignore me. I'm whining.' She waved a dismissive hand. 'I'll find something else. It's just that I really loved my job—and there aren't that many opportunities in the market because there aren't many voiceover studios around.'

He looked interested. 'What does a voiceover studio do?'

'Record jingles for radio stations, produce radio advertising and audio books, and do audio special effects—you know, like horses' hooves or fireworks going off on bonfire night, that kind of thing.'

'So you get all the famous actors and actresses coming in?'

She smiled. 'They're not always household names—but, yeah, I've booked a few in my time.'

'You were in charge of booking?'

'I didn't make the final decisions on who we booked for each job,' Fran said, 'but I made suggestions and I did the organising. I made sure everyone knew what they were supposed to be doing and when.' And she'd fitted in, right smack in the middle of things. She'd *belonged*. And that, to her, had been way more important than her admittedly good salary. 'We had a sales guy handling the sales side of things, a sound manager to do the technical stuff, and my boss did the copywriting and most of the schmoozing.' She bit her lip. 'I'm going to miss it. Horribly. But, hey, life moves on. I'll get over it. Find something else.' She glanced at her watch. 'Sorry. I'm making you really late.'

Gio shook his head. 'It's really not a problem, Fran. My evening's my own. Though I do need to clean the machines so they're ready for tomorrow morning—so, if you don't mind me sorting that out while we're talking, come and sit by the bar.'

Fran looked at him properly for the first time. Gio Mazetti would get a definite ten on the scale of gorgeousness. Olive skin, dark straight hair that flopped across his forehead and which he'd obviously pushed back with one hand at various times during the day because it stuck up in places, a sensual mouth—and the most stunning eyes. With his colouring and his Italian name, she'd expected them to be dark brown. Instead, they were blue.

A mesmerising deep, almost midnight, blue.

She followed him to the bar.

'So when do you finish?' he asked.

That was what had knocked her for six. 'It all happened

today and I cleared my desk this afternoon. I'm on five months' gardening leave, as of now,' she said.

'Five months is pretty generous,' he commented, starting to strip down the coffee machine.

'I worked at the studio for five years, so I guess the terms are one month for every year I spent there,' she explained. 'But the terms of my leave also mean that I can't contact any of my former clients during those five months.'

'So if you go to a competitor, you can't take your contacts with you.'

He'd hit the nail right on the head, and Fran's spirits took another nosedive. 'In five months' time, my contacts will be out of date, because things change so quickly in advertising and radio and publishing. And that's assuming I can get another job in a voiceover studio—as I said, it's not that huge an industry, so even in London there aren't many openings.' She shrugged. 'On the plus side, my skills are transferable. I dunno. Maybe I'll try some of the advertising agencies, see if I can work on the client management side. *If* that doesn't break the terms of my gardening leave, that is.'

'Tell me about what your job involved,' Gio said.

'I kept the schedule for the studios so I knew which slots were free if we were doing a rush job, and which actor was working on which job. I used to talk to the radio stations and audio publishers to sort out timescales, and to the agencies so we had the right voice for the right job. Plus a bit of PA work for the boss and keeping up to date with invoicing and payments.'

'Hmm.' He finished cleaning the machines and leaned on the counter opposite her. 'So you're good at organisation and you're used to keeping track of lots of different projects at the same time, and dealing with lots of different people at lots of different levels.'

That pretty much summed it up. And there was no point in false modesty: she might as well get used to stating what her skills were. She needed the practice for interviews. 'Yes.'

'And you understand finances.'

There was a difference between being honest and sexing it up. She wasn't going to claim to be an accountancy whiz-kid. 'I can do basic book-keeping and set up spreadsheets and produce graphs,' she said.

'Can you read a P and L statement?'

'Profit and loss? Um—I might need to ask some questions, but, yes, I think so.'

'And you understand how profit margins work, the difference between fixed and variable costs?'

She nodded.

He smiled. 'Excellent. In that case, I might have a proposition for you.'

'What sort of proposition?'

'A business proposition.'

Well, of course—it wouldn't be anything else, would it? Some of the actors at the studio had flirted mildly with her, but Fran knew from experience that men basically saw her as a colleague or a friend, not as dating material. She was the one they came to asking for help to woo the girl of their dreams, rather than being the girl who'd caught their eye in the first place. And she was fine with that. Right now her life was complicated enough, without adding in all the muddle of a romantic entanglement.

'It's something that might solve a problem for both of us,' he added mysteriously. 'Have dinner with me tonight and I'll explain.'

Dinner? Didn't he have a wife and family waiting for him at home?

The question must have been written over her face, because his smile broadened. 'Before you ask, I'm single. My *nonna* says that no girl in her right mind will sit around waiting for a workaholic to notice her existence. She also says it's time I settled down, before I hit thirty and I'm on the shelf.' He laughed. 'I've seriously been considering telling her I'm gay.'

A *frisson* of disappointment slid down Fran's spine. Where a gorgeous man was concerned, there was always a rule of three: he'd been snapped up at an early age, he was a rat, or he was gay.

'But apart from the fact I'm not—'

Oh. Not attached and not gay. So did that put him into the rat category?

'—she wouldn't believe me anyway. Because I'm a hopeless liar,' he added with a rueful smile.

So maybe the rule of three didn't apply in this case. Gio might just be the exception that proved the rule.

He smiled at her. 'Don't look so worried. What I'm trying to say is that you're safe with me. I'm not trying to hit on you.'

Which was true, Gio thought—up to a point. He'd noticed Fran Marsden weeks ago. There was something about her: she was quiet, maybe even a little shy, but she always knew exactly what she wanted instead of dithering over the menu, always had the right money, and always had a smile for the barista who made her cappuccino, not taking the service for granted. Efficient and courteous. He liked that. So he'd made a point of working a morning shift in the Charlotte Street café on Wednesdays, when he knew she'd be in; even if he hadn't served her himself, seeing her put a sparkle into the middle of his week.

But he'd never intended to act on that attraction. He knew

better than to mix business with pleasure, and he'd never overstep the boundaries with a customer.

Besides, Nonna was right. There was no point in asking her out because no woman would put up with the hours he worked. And it wasn't fair to suggest a relationship to someone who was just trying to pick up the pieces of her life after some bad news. Especially the way he was feeling right now—restless, at the point where the chain of coffee shops had stopped being a challenge and started being a burden. Though he'd invested so much of his life in Giovanni's, he had no idea what he wanted to do instead.

Except...

No. That particular dream had crashed and burned. He wasn't going back.

But if the idea that had been spinning round in his head for the last few months worked out, he could help Fran pick up the pieces and maybe help stop his restlessness at the same time.

He knew he was acting on impulse, but he'd always been a good judge of character in the past. And he was pretty sure that Fran Marsden was just the kind of woman he needed to help him. 'I think this could be good for both of us,' he said. 'So, will you have dinner with me this evening? I happen to know the best pizzeria in London.'

'Pizza,' she said, the tiniest sparkle in her eyes.

He laughed. 'Well, what else would an Italian suggest for dinner?'

To his pleasure, the sparkle turned into a full-wattage twinkle. And, lord, she was lovely when she smiled properly. It lit her up from the inside, transforming her from average to beautiful.

'Grilled scamorza,' she said. 'Panna cotta. And dough balls with garlic butter.'

Oh, *yes*. A woman on his wavelength. One who actually enjoyed food instead of nibbling at a celery leaf and claiming she was too full to manage anything more—one who saw the pleasure in sharing a meal instead of the misery of counting calories. One who might just understand what he wanted to do. 'That,' he said, 'sounds pretty much perfect. So we have a deal? I'll feed you and you'll listen to what I have to say?'

She shook her head. 'I might not have a job right now, but I can still pay my way. We'll split the bill.'

Not a yes woman, either; he warmed to her even more. Fran was exactly what he was looking for. 'Deal,' he said. He still had a pile of paperwork to do, but he'd done the banking an hour before and the float would be fine in the safe. 'Let me lock up, and we'll go.'

CHAPTER TWO

TWENTY minutes later, Fran and Gio were sitting in a tiny Italian restaurant in Fitzrovia, halfway between Euston Road and Gower Street. The décor was classic: a black-and-white chequered floor, walls colour-washed in amber, marble-topped bistro tables, wrought-iron chairs with thick burgundy-coloured pads on the seats, a chalk board with the day's specials written in European-looking handwriting, and candles set in raffia-covered chianti bottles.

Gio was clearly known here, because the waiter bantered with him before showing them to what looked like the best table in the house.

'So, are you a regular here?' she asked.

'This place does the best food in London. It's where my family comes for birthdays, red-letter days and every other excuse we can think of.'

The waiter materialised beside them and handed them a menu. 'Except you're always late for dinner, Gio, because you're busy working and you have no idea of time. Nonna would tell me to box your ears.'

Gio laughed. 'Ah, now, Marco, she would also tell you that the customer is always right.'

'*You* don't count as a customer,' Marco said, laughing back.

'But you, *signorina*, do.' He set a plate of tiny canapés in between them. 'Don't let him talk you into giving him your share.'

'As if I would—oh…' Gio's eyes widened '…don't eat those cheese discs, Fran. They're inedible. Better let me handle them.'

Marco pretended to cuff him. 'I'll be back in a minute for your order. And behave yourself, or I'll tell Mama what you just said about her cooking.' He winked, and left them with the menus.

'Are the cheese discs really…?' Fran asked, eyeing the plate of gorgeous-looking canapés.

'No, they're fabulous. They're my favourite and I was teasing you. Actually, I was trying to be greedy,' Gio admitted with a smile. 'I'm sorry. I should have said—Marco's my cousin.'

She glanced at the waiter, who was serving another table; now Gio had mentioned it, she could see the family resemblance. But although Marco was good looking and charming, there was something else about Gio. Something that all the other women in the room had clearly noticed, too, because Fran could see just how many heads he'd turned.

'Marco's mother—my Aunt Annetta—is the chef.' Gio's smile turned slightly wry. 'I'm afraid my family's terribly stereotyped.'

'How do you mean?'

'My grandparents moved to London from Milan in the 1950s, and they opened a trattoria,' he explained. 'Their children all went into catering, too—Dad opened a coffee shop, Netti started the pizzeria, and my Uncle Nando is the family ice-cream specialist. He makes the best *gelati* in London.'

'And you're all still close?'

'As I said, we're stereotyped. Typical Italian family.' He spread his hands. 'Big and noisy and knowing way too much of each other's business. Dad, Netti and Nando all live in the same street—the same place I grew up with my sisters and my cousins. Though none of us lives at home now; my generation's spread a bit.' He shrugged. 'Sometimes it feels a bit crowded, and it drives me crazy when they try to organise my social life and find me the perfect girlfriend. But if things get rough it's good to know there's a bunch of people looking out for you, people you can rely on.'

Fran suppressed the feeling of wistfulness before it had a chance to take hold, and tried one of the tiny discs. 'Oh, *wow*.'

Gio smiled. 'Told you they were good.'

'Do you recommend anything in particular?' she asked, scanning the menu.

'Netti's a genius in the kitchen. You could pick anything and it'd taste superb. But you mentioned grilled scamorza, panna cotta and dough balls.'

'They're not on the menu,' Fran pointed out.

'For us, they will be.' He said it without a trace of arrogance; it sounded more like he knew he was getting special treatment, and appreciated it. 'Would you prefer red or white wine?'

'White, please.'

'Pinot grigio all right?'

'Lovely, thanks.'

When Marco returned to take their order, Gio leaned back against his chair and gave him a wicked smile. 'Ah, *cugino mio*. In fact, oh, best cousin in the world—best cousin in the universe…'

Marco groaned. 'You're going to ask for a Giovanni special, aren't you?'

'Yup.' Gio spoke in rapid Italian. Fran couldn't follow the conversation at all, but Gio's accent was incredibly sexy. And he had the most gorgeous mouth. Even when he wasn't talking, there was a permanent tilt to the corner of his lips, as if he were smiling. A real knee-buckler of a smile, too. Yet, at the same time, there was a sense of suppressed energy and restlessness about him. Gio Mazetti was a puzzle. And she found herself wanting to know more about him.

'*Basta*—enough. I'll ask. But as you're her favourite nephew…' Marco rolled his eyes.

'I'm Netti's *only* nephew,' Gio corrected with a grin.

'As I said. Her favourite. So there's a pretty good chance she'll say yes.' Marco smiled. 'One bottle of pinot grigio and a jug of iced water coming up.'

'What's a Giovanni special?' Fran asked.

'Ah.' Gio coughed. 'It's just the topping I like on my pizza. I went through an—um—let's say *experimental* phase in my teens. This one stuck.'

'Experimental?'

'Blue cheese—preferably dolcelatte—and mushrooms.'

She frowned. 'That doesn't sound particularly experimental.'

'No. That would be the other ingredient,' he said drily.

She was intrigued now. 'Which is?'

'Avocado.'

She blinked. 'Avocado on *pizza*? Cooked avocado?'

'Don't knock it until you've tried it,' he advised.

He was full of energy, full of ideas, a little offbeat—and the more time Fran spent with Gio, the more she liked him. His good humour was infectious.

What she couldn't work out was why he'd asked her to dinner. What his proposition was going to be.

When the wine arrived, he didn't bother tasting it; simply thanked Marco, poured out two glasses, and raised his own in a toast to Fran. 'To us—and the beginning of what's going to be a beautiful friendship.' Again, that mischievous half-smile appeared. 'Horribly corny. But it's true anyway. I think we're going to suit each other.'

'How do you mean?' she asked, slightly suspicious.

'I'm sure you're used to dealing with confidential material at the studio,' he said. At her nod, he asked, 'So I trust you'll keep my confidence now?'

'Of course.'

'OK.' He took a deep breath. 'I'm at the point in the business where I need to make some decisions about expansion—either I can open more branches or I can franchise Giovanni's so we open outlets in other cities besides London. There's a fair bit of day-to-day admin in running a chain of coffee shops, so I need to free up some of my time to let me move the business forward.'

It all sounded perfectly logical.

'So I need to find someone who has fabulous organisational skills. Someone who'll be able to be my number two in the business, who can take over from me in juggling rotas and sorting out time management issues, maybe hiring temps or talking people into doing overtime if we have staff off sick. Someone who can sort out the admin, ring the engineers if one of the coffee machines breaks down, help keep the team motivated and not be fazed by dealing with figures and statistics. Someone who's fantastic on the phone and good with people.'

A new challenge. One where she'd be working with people. Using all her skills. This sounded right up her street.

As if he'd read her mind, he added softly, 'And I think that person's you.'

'You've only just met me. How do you know I'm what you're looking for?' she asked. 'For all you know, I'm not

really an experienced office manager. I could be a pathological liar.'

'I've worked in this business long enough to be a good
judge of people,' he said simply. 'I trust my instinct. You're
no bunny-boiler. And if you were a pathological liar, you'd
have told me that not only could you read a P and L statement, you could do business projection modelling and write
your own computer programs, while juggling six flaming
torches and tap-dancing on a tightrope all at the same time.'

She couldn't help smiling at the picture he'd painted.
'Juggling, tap-dancing and tightrope walking aren't quite my
forte. Though I can use a computer and I know where to get
help if I'm stuck.'

'Exactly. You're straight and practical and honest.'

Which wasn't quite what a woman wanted to hear from a
man, but this wasn't a date anyway, she reminded herself. This
was business.

'In short, you're exactly what I'm looking for.' He paused.
'Though, since you brought it up, how do you know that *I'm*
not a pathological liar?'

'Because if you didn't own or at least run the coffee shop,
you wouldn't have been the only one there after closing time,
you wouldn't have the keys and you probably wouldn't be
called Giovanni.'

'He isn't. His real name's Fred,' Marco interposed,
bringing them the scamorza.

'Just ignore him. He's only jealous because his coffee's
not as good as mine,' Gio retorted with a grin. '*Cugino mio*,
any time you want a lesson on getting the perfect crema on
an espresso—'

'—I'll ask your dad,' Marco teased. 'Enjoy your *antipasto*,
signorina…?' He waited for a name.

'Fran,' she said with a smile.

'Fran.' He looked thoughtful. 'Short for Frances?'

'Francesca.'

'An Italian name. Hmm.' Marco gave Gio a knowing look, and was rewarded with a stream of Italian.

Fran, judging it wiser not to ask, tried her scamorza. 'It's gorgeous,' she said.

'Course it is. My aunt Netti's a fabulous cook.' Gio gave her another of those knee-buckling smiles. 'So, Fran. *Francesca*. Your family has Italian blood?'

'No idea.' And she really wasn't comfortable talking about her family.

He didn't seem upset that she'd been a bit short with him. 'So we've established that we trust each other, yes?'

She wasn't quite sure how to answer that.

'Trust has to start somewhere,' he said softly. 'And if you see the best in people—expect the best from them—they'll give you their best.'

'Is this another of your Italian grandmother's sayings?'

'Yup—she's a very wise woman, my *nonna*. When I was a teenager, I used to think she was just rabbiting on. But, the older I get, the more I realise she knows what she's talking about.' He raised an eyebrow. 'Actually, you remind me of her in a way.'

'I'll take that as a compliment.'

'It was.' He ate another mouthful of scamorza. 'As I said, this job's got your name on it. But you'll also need to understand the business from the bottom up.'

'Running a coffee shop?'

He nodded. 'Specifically, Giovanni's. What makes us different from the competition. What makes us special. What makes people come to us instead of one of the national chains or the independents. So I need someone who understands about coffee.'

Fran shook her head. 'That counts me out. I know what I like—cappuccino and latte—but when it comes to all these complicated orders…'

Gio took a sip of wine. 'Firstly, all coffees are based on espresso. And Giovanni's doesn't go in for coffee that takes half an hour and a degree in rocket science to order. We make it easy for the customer. A basic espresso for those who like black coffee; latte, cappuccino and Americano for those who like varying degrees of milk or frothiness. Hot chocolate, mocha for those who like a mixture, tea with milk or lemon, and iced coffees and smoothies in summer.' He ticked them off on his fingers. 'Pastries and biscotti in the morning, paninis for lunch and cakes for the middle of the afternoon. It's a matter of knowing what our customers like and second-guessing the right quantities so that we don't run out, but also don't have to throw away too much.' He looked thoughtful. 'I suppose it's like you'd book your studio slots so you weren't empty half the time and double-booked the rest of the time.'

She could appreciate that. But the coffee thing… 'I don't even have an espresso machine at home.'

He groaned. 'Don't tell me you drink instant coffee?'

'No, I use a cafetiere. Same at work—well, used to,' she corrected herself. She really had to get her head round the fact that she didn't work at the voiceover studio any more. 'I like my coffee fresh, not stuck in a filter pot stewing for half a day.'

'Then you already have a feel for what we do. Fran, the best way to understand a business is to work in it for a while—and I'm short-staffed right now. I'm about to lose one of my baristas because she wants to go travelling.'

She flinched. 'Like my boss.'

He smiled ruefully. 'I'm sorry. I didn't mean to rub salt in your wounds. But—to quote Nonna yet again—when one door closes, another opens. This is an opportunity for both of us. I need someone with your skills, and you're on garden leave for five months. It strikes me you're the sort who enjoys being busy and rises to a challenge, so if you work with me this will solve both our problems. I get an office manager who can take some of the weight off me and let me plan where to go next with the business and maybe let me bounce ideas off her, and you get a job that you can stretch to suit you.'

It sounded as if he had it all worked out.

'And the coffee thing isn't a problem. I can train you as a barista, teach you what you need to know. If you work a few shifts in one of the coffee shops, you'll understand the business more and you'll be able to bring that to the office manager job too.' He looked thoughtful. 'You'll need a food hygiene certificate, but the course only takes a few hours and the exam's pretty straightforward.'

Exams? Oh, no. This was where it all went pear-shaped. 'I'm not good at exams,' she told him. 'I tend panic. I failed my A levels.'

'But in day-to-day practical things, you're fine.'

It was a statement, not a question. She nodded.

'Then think of the exam as just another day-to-day practical thing.'

'That's what my parents said about the driving test. It still took me four goes—and Suzy and the twins all passed theirs first time.'

'Suzy and the twins?' he asked.

She shifted in her seat. 'I'm the eldest of four.' Sort of.

'The same as me.' He smiled. 'Now I know why you're

brilliantly organised. You've had years of practice, bossing your siblings about.'

'They're a trainee dentist, a PhD student and a forensic scientist. Bossing them about wouldn't work,' she said with a rueful smile. They were all academic and brilliant at exams, unlike her. They all excelled in sports, too, had always been picked for the school's first team, whereas she'd been hopeless—in sixth form she'd opted to do voluntary work at the local old people's home on Wednesday afternoons rather than sports.

She was the eldest. And most definitely the odd one out.

Probably because she didn't share the same gene pool.

Marco took away their empty plates and returned with pizza and a bowl of salad. 'Mama says panna cotta would take too long, but crème brûlée is on the specials board and she can do you some with raspberries.'

'Fabulous.' Gio smiled. 'Tell her she's the joint best mother in the world, along with mine.'

'Tell her yourself. There are big hints in the kitchen that she hasn't seen her favourite nephew for months.'

'It hasn't been anywhere near that long,' Gio protested.

'Eat your pizza. Then go see Mama, if you want pudding,' Marco advised. 'Fran, would you like pepper? Parmesan?'

'I'm fine, thanks.' She smiled back at him.

'*Bene*. Enjoy,' he said, and left them to it.

'You have to try this,' Gio insisted, and cut a small piece from his pizza. 'Here.' He offered her a forkful across the table; it felt oddly intimate, leaning across to take a bite, and when her gaze met his she felt a weird shifting in the region of her heart, as if it had just turned a somersault.

Oh, lord. Don't say she was falling for Gio Mazetti, a man she barely knew and who was just about to become her boss?

'Well?' he asked. 'So what do you think of avocado on pizza?'

'It's…different.'

He laughed. 'That's the diplomatic answer.'

She shifted the conversation back to business before it drifted on to personal ground. *Dangerous* ground. Because if she was going to work with Gio, any other sort of relationship was definitely out of the question. 'You said you were thinking of expanding or franchising. How big is Giovanni's?'

'We have four outlets in London,' he said. 'So I'm at the stage where I need to decide what to do next. Well, I say "I".' He waved a dismissive hand. 'Dad started the business.'

'But you're in charge now.'

He nodded. 'Though I need to consider Dad's feelings. Franchising's a possibility, but I need to do some proper research into what it all means and whether it's the right way for us to go. And at the moment I simply don't have the time.'

The pizzeria was another of his family's businesses, and his aunt was clearly still hands on. Gio's father couldn't be that much older than Annetta, surely; so why wasn't he hands-on with the coffee shop? 'You seem—well, pretty young to be heading a chain of coffee shops,' she commented.

'I'm twenty-eight. But I've worked in the business for half my life. And I learned how to make decent espresso at my father's knee.'

'And because you're the eldest, you were groomed to take over from your dad?'

For a brief moment, his face was filled with bleakness. And then, before she had the chance to ask him what was wrong, he smiled. 'Something like that.'

She was pretty sure there was something he wasn't telling her. 'Your *nonna* said that trust has to start somewhere,' she reminded him softly. 'So why don't you fill me in on the story?'

He toyed with his pizza for a while before answering. 'I planned to go to college, ten years ago. I was going to study music. I helped out in the business while I was at school—we all did, whether it was washing up or baristaing or clearing the tables for Dad and washing them down when the shop closed—but this one night I was meant to be working a late shift when I had a chance to play in a concert. A concert where I knew a scout for a record company was going to be in the audience. Dad said I had to follow my dreams, and he'd do my shift for me, even though he'd been working all day and it meant he'd be doing a double shift. I was eighteen. Head full of stars. So I went. I played. The scout had a word with me and my guitar teacher. And I came home by the coffee shop to tell Dad my news.' He dragged in a breath. 'Which was when I found him lying on the floor. He'd had a heart attack while he was shutting up the shop. The ambulance got there in time to save him, but no way was I going to make Dad cope with the stress of the business after that.'

'So you gave up music to take over from him?' she guessed.

He grimaced. 'I probably wasn't good enough to make it commercially anyway. There isn't that much scope for a classical guitarist.' He spread his hands. 'A bit of session work, a bit of teaching, the occasional gig in some arts club. It's a bits-and-pieces sort of life, whereas running Giovanni's means I can do pretty much what I like, when I like. It wasn't a hard choice.'

The momentary flicker in those blue, blue eyes told her that he was lying. That even now he wondered, *what if?* But it hadn't stopped him making the decision. He'd given up his dreams for his family.

Fran realised with a pang that Gio was the kind of man who believed in commitment. Who believed in his family.

A belief she so wanted to have. Except she didn't share his certainty in belonging, the way that he did. Even though her parents had told her years before that she was special, that they'd chosen her to be part of their family, she wasn't sure she belonged. Because they'd chosen her when they didn't think they could have their own children, and she'd always thought that they regretted their decision when it turned out to be not the case. It was an unspoken fear, but one that still surfaced from time to time. Like now, when she'd stopped fitting in at work and she'd been the one to be made redundant rather than the other office manager.

Gio came from a large family. One that teased and drove him crazy, but clearly loved him to bits. If she accepted his offer of a job, would she fit in to his world any better than she fitted into her family?

'What was the news?' she asked. 'The news you called by to tell him?'

Gio took a sip of wine. 'Nothing important.'

She didn't quite believe him. Hadn't he said that the scout had had a word with him? But she had a feeling that if she pushed, Gio would clam up completely.

'Besides, I've enjoyed managing the coffee shop. Dad believed in me enough to let me run it without interference. The one on Charlotte Street is the original café, but he was fine about me expanding it.' He looked at her. 'I said earlier about trusting people. I also need to be honest with you. Right now, it's not so much the business that's at a crossroads, it's me.' He sighed. 'I don't know whether it's because I'm heading towards thirty—a kind of early midlife crisis—but right now I feel in limbo. I don't know what I want from life.

And I need to find out while I'm still young enough to do something about it.'

That accounted for the suppressed restlessness she'd spotted earlier. 'Music?' she asked. Did he want to follow the dream he'd given up ten years before?

'I'm too old. Too out of practice. I only play for myself nowadays, anyway.' He shook his head. 'I don't know. I can promise you one thing, though—I'm not intending to sell the business or make you redundant. I just need…time. To sort a few things out in my head. And I need someone to help me. Someone to give me that time.'

He needed someone.

And he'd asked her.

'How about we have a month's trial, with a week's notice on either side?' she asked.

The smile he gave her was like that of a drowning man who'd just been thrown a lifeline. 'Sounds good to me. When do you want to start?'

CHAPTER THREE

'How about tomorrow?' The words came out before he could stop them. Too eager. Stupid, Gio berated himself mentally. If he wasn't careful, he'd scare her off.

'Straight from one job to another, without a break?' she asked, raising an eyebrow.

Very stupid, he amended silently. Hell. Now she was going to say no. Because he'd rushed her. Of course she'd want a break between jobs. Time to recharge her batteries. Would he never learn not to jump in feet first?

And then she smiled. 'Well, it beats sitting around feeling sorry for myself. Tomorrow it is.'

He could've kissed her. Except officially, they were working together now. And Gio had seen too many good business relationships messed up when sex had got in the way of business. He wasn't going to make that mistake. Even though he was definitely attracted to Fran and every time he looked at her he felt that low, humming excitement in his blood.

A feeling he'd just have to keep in check.

He settled on taking her hand and shaking it, instead. 'Thanks. You have no idea how much I appreciate this.'

Time to let her hand go, now.

Now.

Because this was teetering on the very fine line between being a handshake and holding her hand. And he was aware of a tingling in his palm where her skin touched his.

This wasn't the time. And in the middle of his aunt's restaurant was definitely not the place. As it was, Marco had assumed that Fran was his girlfriend, and despite Gio's denial the family grapevine was probably already buzzing.

He knew he'd get a call from his mother tonight, asking him how come he'd taken his girlfriend to meet his Aunt Netti before meeting his mother. Not to mention texts from Bella, Jude and Marcie staking their claims as bridesmaids, demanding full details of their new sister-in-law-to-be, and offering dinner invitations so they could meet her and grill her for themselves: his family didn't seem to believe in taking things slowly.

Just as well he'd switched his mobile phone to 'discreet' mode. Pity he couldn't switch his family to 'discreet' in the same way.

'Appreciate what?' Marco asked, overhearing Gio's last comment.

Gio resisted the temptation to wring his cousin's neck, and let go of Fran's hand. 'Perfect timing, *cugino mio*. I'd like you to meet my new office manager.'

Marco stared at Fran, and then at Gio. 'Office manager?'

'Yup.'

'You're telling me you've just been conducting a job interview—over dinner?' Disbelief filled every note of his cousin's voice.

'It's the civilised way to do things.' Gio gave a wry smile. 'And as I have to eat anyway…'

'You decided to multi-task it.' Marco made exaggerated quote marks with his fingers around the word 'multi-task', and rolled his eyes. 'You're unbelievable. Fran, he did warn you he's a workaholic and his favourite phrase is "multi-task it", didn't he? Don't let him take advantage of you.'

'She's too efficient to do that,' Gio retorted.

Fran coughed. 'And I'm also quite capable of speaking for myself, thank you very much.'

'Indeed. And I apologise, Fran. My family's bad habit—' well, one of them, Gio thought '—is that we talk too much.' He spread his hands. 'Speaking of which…I'd better sneak into the kitchen to see my aunt. If you'll excuse me for a little while?' No way was he taking Fran with him to meet Netti. He needed to stop the family rumours before they spread: and he didn't want his new office manager frightened off by the idea of his family claiming her as his new girlfriend.

Which she wasn't.

Because he didn't have a girlfriend.

Didn't want a girlfriend.

Didn't *need* a girlfriend.

OK, so his life wasn't absolutely perfect at the moment. He couldn't shift this restlessness, this feeling that there was a black hole in the middle of his life. He had no idea what he was looking for or what might fill that black hole—but he was pretty sure that it wasn't settling down, getting married and having babies, whatever his family might think.

The second he walked into the kitchen, he was greeted with a hug and then a cuff round the ear by his aunt.

'I'm too old and—at nearly a foot taller than you—too big for that,' he said with a grin.

'That's what you'd like to think. I'm older and wiser and I know better. So where is she, then?' Annetta asked.

'Who?'

'This *bella ragazza* Marco's told me about. Francesca. This nice Italian girl.'

'Netti, *dolcezza*, you know I adore you. But you're jumping to conclusions.' He kissed her cheek. 'First of all, Fran's not Italian.'

'With a name like Francesca?' Annetta scoffed. 'Come off it.'

'She's not Italian,' Gio repeated. 'Secondly, she happens to be my new office manager. You lot have been nagging me for months and months and months to pace myself and take some time off—aren't you pleased that I'm finally taking your advice and hiring myself some help?'

But his aunt refused to be diverted. 'Marco says she's nice. She has a pretty smile. And that you don't look at her as if she's a colleague.'

'Yes, she's nice,' Gio agreed. 'But Marco's just become a dad and he's sleep-deprived. He's seeing things that aren't there. She's my *colleague*. And I'm not looking to settle down.'

'You're not even looking at going out with anyone, let alone settling down! And you need a social life as well as your work,' Annetta said, pursing her lips. 'You need someone to take you in hand. Why not this so-called "new office manager" of yours?'

'Because.' Gio knew better than to get drawn into this argument. He'd be here all night. 'Netti, *cara*, I should get back to Fran, before she decides I'm going to be a terrible boss and changes her mind. And Marco did say you'd made us crème brûlée with raspberries…'

'Don't think you're getting out of it that easily,' his aunt warned, but she smiled and handed him the two dessert dishes. 'Ring your mother tonight. You don't call her enough. And you work too hard.'

'*Sì, mia zia.* I know. That's the way I'm made. It's how Mazetti men are.'

She threw up her hands. 'You're impossible.'

He kissed her cheek. 'Thanks for the pudding.'

'My pleasure, *piccolo.*' She shooed him towards the door. 'Off you go, then. Back to the *bella ragazza.*'

Uh-oh. She clearly hadn't listened to a word he'd said. That, or she'd decided not to believe him. 'Please remember, Netti, Fran's my office manager, *not* my girlfriend. Whatever you, my mother or Nonna would like to think—or dream up between the three of you,' he said.

Annetta laughed. 'You can tell Nonna that yourself. You know she's coming over from Milan in about three weeks.'

'I'm not sure,' Gio said, 'whether that's a threat or a promise.' He laughed, and fled from the kitchen before his aunt could flick a wet tea-towel at him.

Gio placed the dish of crème brûlée in front of Fran. 'This will be the best you've ever tasted,' he told her.

It certainly looked good. 'How was your aunt?' she asked politely.

'Fine. I was told off for not taking you to meet her. But...' He shook his head. 'As one of four kids, you've got a better chance than most people of coping with the Mazettis. But you've only just agreed to be my office manager. I don't want them scaring you off before you've even started.'

'How would they do that?'

'The women are—how can I put this nicely?—bossy. I grew up in a house with four women, so I can just about hold my own with my mother and my sisters—and my aunt. But when they add Nonna to the mix...' He groaned. 'She's coming over from Milan in three weeks' time. So I'm going to have to go into hiding.'

'Your grandmother's really that scary?'

'No-o. Not exactly. She's very straightforward—she tends to tell things like they are. I don't think you'd have a problem with that. But…' he sighed '…as I said, she's got this thing about wanting me to settle down. Mum and Netti are her sidekicks, and they've got Marco on the team now—his wife had a little girl two weeks ago, and he's just besotted with his wife and daughter. He thinks I should do what he's done: find the perfect wife for me and have babies.'

He looked utterly horrified at the idea.

So was he the odd one out in his family, too? The one who didn't want to do what all the others had done?

She smiled wryly. 'I suppose that's the good thing about being from a family of academics. Nobody expects you to settle down until you're at least thirty. So I'm safe for the next four years or so.'

'Is that what you want?' Gio asked. 'To settle down and have babies?'

A family to belong to. Where she'd fit smack into the middle of things. Be the hub.

She suppressed the shiver of longing. 'Right now, I'm quite happy being single and fancy-free,' she said lightly.

'Hallelujah. Finally I've found someone female who's on my wavelength—who actually understands where I'm coming from. You're going to be on my side on this, right?' Gio raised his glass to her. 'To us. And we're going to make a brilliant team.'

The pudding was indeed the best Fran had ever tasted. The coffee was good, too. And when they'd settled the bill and left the pizzeria, she was shocked to realise how late it was—how long she'd been chatting to Gio at the restaurant.

A man she'd only just met.

And yet, weirdly, it felt as if she'd known him for years. She couldn't remember feeling so comfortable with someone so soon—ever.

'I'll see you home,' Gio said.

She shook her head. 'Thanks, but there's really no need. I can look after myself.'

'Remember, I was brought up the Italian way—it doesn't feel right just to abandon you at the door of my aunt's pizzeria and let you find your own way home. Let me at least walk you to the Tube station.' Clearly he sensed that she was about to refuse, because he added, 'Besides, we need to discuss when you're going to start tomorrow and which branch, so we might as well—'

'—multi-task it,' she finished.

His eyes crinkled at the corners. 'See. You can even read my mind.'

'Hardly. Marco did tell me it was your favourite phrase,' she reminded him with a smile. 'OK. As long as it's not taking you out of your way.'

'I live within walking distance of the station,' he said. 'And it's a warm, dry evening. The fresh air will do me good.'

By the time he'd walked her to Goodge Street station, they'd agreed to meet at the coffee shop on Charlotte Street at half past nine, and she'd checked the dress code—the baristas all wore black trousers or skirts and a white shirt, so she'd do the same. Gio insisted on waiting with her on the platform until she'd got on to the Tube, and then sketched a wave before striding off again.

When one door closes, another opens.

And how. She'd lost her dream job, stared failure in the face, then only a few hours later, she'd been offered something that might turn out to be even better. Something where she'd have free rein.

Gio was prepared to take a chance on her. So she'd take a chance on him. And she had a month to find out if she'd made the right choice.

The following morning, Gio had just finished signing for a delivery when Fran walked in.

He was used to seeing her on a Wednesday morning—but not this early, and only for the couple of minutes it took her to order her cappuccino and almond croissant. Seeing her now and knowing that she was going to be spending the day in his office, sitting at his desk, in his chair, felt...weird.

'Good morning,' she said.

Lord, she had the sweetest smile. A smile that did things to him. Things he hadn't expected. He tried to ignore the flutter at the base of his spine and strove for casualness. 'Hi.'

'Sorry I'm a bit early.'

'Well, you have to make a good impression on your first day,' he teased. He introduced her swiftly to the baristas. 'This is Fran. She's our new office manager. And, no, before you ask, it *doesn't* mean you can all go swanning off inter-railing like Kelly and let me cover your shifts.'

Sally clicked her fingers. 'Damn. And there I was, planning to spend the summer on a beach full of gorgeous Italian men.'

Gio laughed. 'That's easy. Just go to one of my family's back gardens on a Sunday afternoon.'

'A sandpit and a horde of boys under the age of seven isn't *quite* the same thing, Gio.'

'They're male, Italian and gorgeous, yes?'

She groaned. 'Yes.'

'And there's sand.'

'But no sea.'

'That's a minor detail. Plus, everyone has a freezer full of Nando's best ice cream. What more do you need?' he teased.

Sally rolled her eyes. 'Welcome to the madhouse, Fran.'

'Thanks. I think.' Fran smiled back.

'Let me show you round,' Gio said. He gave her a tour of the coffee shop, then showed her into the small staff kitchen, rest room and office at the back of the shop.

Judging by the papers piled in a haphazard mountain on the desk, filing clearly wasn't his thing—and he obviously knew it, because he looked slightly embarrassed. 'I do know where everything is. I'm just not that good at putting things away.'

'And I bet your computer's the same. All the files lumped under one directory.'

'I'm not quite that bad.' Gio's blue eyes softened. 'I've just been too busy lately to keep on top of the filing. I did tell you I needed someone to sort me out. I'll get you a coffee and then I'll talk you through the computer systems.'

He reappeared shortly after with two mugs of coffee.

'You need these.' She handed him an envelope. 'Details for your personnel records.'

He opened the envelope and looked through the files. 'CV, emergency contact details, NI number, bank details—great, thanks—hmm, no, don't need these.' He handed the references back to her without even a cursory scan of the text.

'Why not?'

'The new studio owners are probably going to feel guilty about pushing you out so they'll have written you a very glowing reference to make up for it. On the other hand, they're also too short-sighted to see what they've passed up—so I doubt if their views are worth the paper they're written on.'

He smiled to take the sting from his words. 'Besides, I told you yesterday, I'm a good judge of character. So even though one or two of my baristas came with less-than-glowing reports from previous employers, I went by my gut instinct and I was proved right. They came good.'

'One of your grandmother's sayings?' she guessed.

'If you see the best in people, they'll give you their best.' He nodded. 'Actually, there was one thing we didn't discuss yesterday. Money. You're working for Giovanni's, so you need a salary. What were you on at your last place?'

She told him.

He sighed. 'I can just about match that, but I'm afraid I can't raise it. You'd probably get a lot more from a financial services company or one of the big ad agencies.'

'But you,' she said, 'promised me free rein.'

He smiled. 'I trust you not to make changes just for the sake of it.' He talked her through the different systems on the computer, showing her how the information was coded for each of the four branches and how they fed into an overall system. 'Your username is "marsfran", and this is your password.' He scribbled her initials and a series of numbers on to a piece of paper.

'You sorted this out for me already?'

He shrugged. 'It didn't take long. Besides, I'd left some papers here that I needed last night.' He hadn't stayed particularly long. In peace and quiet with no interruptions, you could get a lot done in a couple of hours. Which was why he was usually in not long after dawn. Before the rush started.

'I'm beginning to see what your cousin means about you being a workaholic,' Fran said dryly.

'Don't tell me you're going over to their team. I need you on my side.' He smiled at her. 'Well, the best way to get used to new systems and what have you is to play with them. If you get stuck, just give me a yell. I'll leave you to it to book yourself on the food hygiene course—the place I normally use is in the address book under "food hygiene course"—and take a look through the systems.'

'And do your filing?' she asked, raising one eyebrow.

Gio pantomimed innocence. 'I didn't ask—but as you've just offered…'

She laughed. 'I'll see what I can do.'

'Give me a yell if you need anything or you get stuck. Otherwise, I'll bring you some coffee and an almond croissant.' He smiled at her. 'I haven't forgotten about the barista training, but the morning rush is probably *not* the best time to introduce you to the delights of the espresso machine and the milk frother. Maybe if there's an afternoon lull? Or just before I strip the machines down after we close?'

'You're the boss,' she said lightly. 'You tell me.'

'Later,' he promised, winked, and left her to it.

The day went surprisingly quickly. Fran sorted out the filing and worked through the different systems, making a list of questions for Gio as she went. He came in a couple of times, bearing a cup of coffee or a cool drink—and one time bringing her a list of what he needed ordering from the suppliers for delivery to each branch, the following morning—but for the most part she was on her own in Gio's office.

The wallpaper on his computer screen was a family photograph. His parents, she guessed, plus three younger women who had to be his sisters, and an older woman who was probably his Italian grandmother. Gio was standing right in the middle of them, with a huge smile on his face. Whatever his protests about not wanting to settle down, he clearly loved his family. And he'd given up his dreams for them. He was a man who wasn't afraid to make sacrifices. Who'd give everything for those he loved.

At the end of their shifts, Sally and Ian put their heads round the door to say goodbye. Fran felt a weird glow spread through her. Her first day, and already she was accepted as part of the team. Just as she'd been at the voiceover studio. Maybe this was going to work out just fine.

She logged off the computer, and then Gio walked in. 'Wow. Are you Mary Poppins in disguise? You know, waving a magic wand and everything tidies itself up and marches in the right order into the right file in the right drawer?'

She laughed. 'All you needed was a system. And it wasn't actually that bad. There was a kind of order to the chaos.'

He perched himself on the edge of the desk. 'The office looks better than it has in years. I normally don't let Dad anywhere near here—in his day he kept things absolutely spotless, and seeing it in a mess would be an excuse for him to get back in here and start working stupid hours again.'

Considering the hours Gio worked… 'Like father, like son?'

'But I'm twenty-eight, not fifty-eight. And I haven't had a heart attack.' Gio made a face. 'I just want him to take things easy and not worry.' He waved a dismissive hand. 'But we need to sort out this barista training. We said we'd do it now, after closing, but you were in early this morning. So tomorrow I don't want to see you until eleven, OK?'

She blinked. 'But…'

'No buts.' He held up one hand to forestall any protest. 'Your hours are Monday to Friday, nine to five with an hour for lunch. If you work more than that, you take time in lieu or you fill out an overtime form. I don't expect you to work the same hours I do.'

Reminding her—in a nice way—that he was the boss and she was the employee. And she'd better keep that in mind. This was an employer–employee relationship, nothing else.

'So how's your first day been?' he asked.

'Good,' she said. 'I like Ian and Sally. And the people in the other branches were fine when they spoke to me.'

'That's a point,' Gio said. 'I need to take you to the other cafés so you can meet the staff there, too. Maybe tomorrow afternoon, or Friday morning.'

'So this is where you're based, most of the time?' she asked.

'Most of the time,' Gio agreed. 'Though I try to do a shift in each of the outlets, once a week. It gives the team a chance to talk to me about any problems that need fixing or any suggestions they have for improvements or innovations—and it gives me a chance to make sure everything's ticking over as it should be and there aren't any problems that need sorting before they get unmanageable. But this was the first branch Dad opened, so the office space is here.' He spread his hands. 'Ready to learn what it takes to be a barista?'

'Sure.'

He talked her through how to use the machines and the steps needed to make an espresso. And then it was her turn. Despite taking notes, she'd forgotten one or two points—but Gio was standing behind her, ready to show her what to do. Not close enough to touch, but she was aware of how near his body was to hers. She could almost feel the heat of his body. And when his left arm reached out to the grinder, his bare skin brushed against hers, for just the tiniest fraction of a second, but it felt as if electricity zinged through every nerve-end.

Mentally, she went through the steps. Grind, dose,

tamp—she tapped the filter gently and watched the contents level, then pressed it down as he'd shown her—fit the filter into the machine, flick the switch and let it pour... She counted for twenty seconds in her head, then turned the tap off.

'Looks good,' Gio said, looking over her shoulder. His breath fanned her ear, and she felt a shiver of anticipation run down her back.

Stop it, she warned herself. He's your *boss*.

So why couldn't she stop thinking about him on a personal level? Why couldn't she stop wondering how his mouth would feel against the curve of her neck? Why couldn't she stop thinking how easy it would be to take one tiny step backwards so that her body was in close contact with his, and his arms would curve round her waist, holding her to him...?

'Stir it,' Gio said softly.

She did, half-expecting the coffee to stay black with just a tiny bit of foam clinging to the edges of the cup, but the crema reformed. 'Wow.'

'Now watch and wait.'

She watched as the thousands of tiny, tiny bubbles began to disperse. And as the caramel-coloured foam started to dissolve, so her awareness of Gio's nearness grew. To the point where she was having a seriously hard time keeping her cool. It wasn't that he was invading her personal space—it was that she *wanted* him to.

Which was a seriously bad idea.

He was her new boss.

Which meant hands off.

She'd seen what happened with office romances. The way the working relationship turned so awkward that one of them had to leave—and until that happened everyone was walking on eggshells. Messy. Complicated. Not something she wanted to happen here.

Gio glanced at his watch when the crema had almost vanished. 'Just over a minute. Good. OK, you can do a second one. This time it's for tasting.'

When he'd tasted it, he said, 'Good. Just the right amount of smoothness. Try it.' He held the mug to her lips.

Her mouth was right where his had just touched. Oh, lord. This was getting ridiculous. She'd spent years working without ever falling for a colleague or a client. So why was she reacting this way to Gio? Besides, he probably taught all his baristas this way, standing close to them so he could reach out and guide them where necessary.

This wasn't personal.

It just felt like it.

'Good?' he asked.

'Good.' Her voice sounded very slightly squeaky; she really hoped he hadn't noticed.

'Excellent. Thus endeth your first lesson. We'll do lattes tomorrow.' He smiled at her. 'See you tomorrow. I'm over in Holborn first thing, but you can buzz through to me if you need anything. And I'll take you round the other branches tomorrow afternoon.'

Class most definitely dismissed, Fran thought, even though he'd done it in the most charming way. 'Do you want me to stay and help clean the machines?'

Ouch. That sounded like an attempt to be the teacher's pet.

'No, that's fine. I've kept you here long enough. And, Fran?'

'Yes?'

He smiled at her. 'Thanks. I appreciate what you've done today.'

'No worries. See you later.' She replaced her notebook in

a tray in the office, collected her handbag from the bottom drawer, and lifted her hand in a casual wave goodbye as she left the coffee shop.

Putting distance between herself and Gio Mazetti was a good idea, she thought. And hopefully by the time she saw him again, she'd have it fixed in her head that they were colleagues only—and staying that way.

CHAPTER FOUR

THE next morning, Fran felt awkward going in to work so late—especially as Gio wasn't there—but Sally and Ian, the baristas, greeted her cheerfully enough. Sally had a mug of coffee ready for her just the way she liked it before she'd even reached the office. Gio had emailed her from Holborn, asking if she'd get some information for him about specific aspects of franchising, so she spent the rest of the morning researching, and the afternoon setting up a spreadsheet that would do automated graphs showing the figures for each coffee shop.

She knew the second that Gio walked into the coffee shop; even though she couldn't see him from the office, she was aware of his presence. Something that made the air tingle.

So much for her pep talk, the previous evening, spent in front of the bathroom mirror, repeating over and over again that Gio Mazetti was her boss and way off limits. It wasn't as if she'd been bothered before about being single or on the shelf. Why should things be different now?

'Hi.' He walked into the office and leaned against the edge of her desk. 'Good day so far?'

'Yes. You?'

'Pretty good. I've got a new supplier coming to see us

tomorrow morning—someone who does organic cakes. So we'll need to do a taste test and, if we like it, work out what we're going to have to charge to keep the same profit margin and where the break-even points are. She left me the price list.' He handed her a folder. 'Tomorrow, can you sort me out some suggested figures for a trial?'

'No problem.' She flicked into her tasklist and typed rapidly.

'Thanks. Are you still OK for another half-hour lesson on baristaing, tonight?' he asked.

So he was still going to teach her, not get Sally or one of the others to take over? A warm glow spread through her. 'Sure.' She tried for a light tone. 'This is where I get to do the milk, yes?'

'Yep. Have you got the orders from Holborn and the others?'

'Yes, and I was just about to ring the supplier,' she said with a smile.

He smacked his palm against his forehead. 'Sorry, sorry. I'm teaching you to suck eggs.'

'No. But you've been doing this for years. It must be hard to give up control.'

'A bit,' he admitted. 'You've got your course booked?'

'I was going to ask you about that. I can go on Tuesday or Thursday next week. Which one would fit in best with whatever you've got planned?'

'Either. And I'm not expecting to see you in here before or after, whichever day it is,' he said firmly. 'Straight to college from home—and straight back home from college, OK?'

'Yes, boss.' She saluted him. 'Though I assume you'd like me to let you know if I pass?'

'When,' he corrected. 'Of course you'll pass.'

She'd already told him she wasn't good when it came to exams, so it felt good that he had that much confidence in her.

'When you've phoned the order through, come out the front and I'll take you on a whistle-stop tour of the Giovanni's empire.' He smiled at her, and left her to it.

When she emerged from the office, a few minutes later, she was surprised when Gio led her to a car.

'Wouldn't it be easier to go by Tube?'

'With all those line changes? Even Holborn, all of two stops away, means a line change. If you add in Islington and Docklands...' He grimaced. 'It's a lot less hassle to do it this way.'

The car wasn't what she'd expected, either. It must have shown on her face, because he said with a grin, 'Just what were you expecting me to drive, Fran?'

Well, he'd asked—she might as well be honest. 'A Harley. Or maybe a two-seater.'

He laughed. 'First off, if I had a motorbike, it'd be a Ducati—I'd always pick an Italian make first. But if you've ever tried having a guitar case as your pillion passenger...' For a second, his face clouded. And then he looked wistful. 'A two-seater... Yeah.'

'A Ferrari?' It was the only Italian sports car she could think of.

'Along with taking out a second mortgage to pay for the insurance? No.' He shook his head. 'My first car was a two-seater—an Alfa. I bought her the day after I passed my driving test. Dad went bananas that I'd spent so much money on an old car with a soft top that always leaked, but she was the love of my life. The day the mechanic told me there was no way he'd be able to fix her up to pass the MOT and I'd have to scrap her...' He sighed. 'I rang every car museum I could think of to see if I could donate her somewhere she'd get a kind retirement.'

'And you found somewhere?'

'No.' He opened the passenger door of the estate car for her. 'Dad had to take her to the scrap dealer's for me. I couldn't face it.'

Oh, bless. On impulse, she gave him a hug.

And then wished she hadn't when every single nerve-end started tingling.

And tingled a bit more when Gio's arms came round her to return the hug. 'Thank you,' he said. 'For not laughing at me.'

'Course I wouldn't laugh at you,' she said, hoping her voice didn't sound as rough and croaky to him as it did to her, and she ducked into the car.

She just about managed to recover her composure by the time he slid into the driving seat. 'So how come you've got an estate car now?' It was the complete opposite of a little two-seater sports car.

'Because Marco got really fed up with me borrowing his to do the cash-and-carry run, and nagged me into getting my own. Although my suppliers deliver nowadays, I haven't got round to changing the car to something a bit smaller and easier to park.' He slanted her a look. 'Don't tell me you drive a two-seater?'

'I don't have a car.' She shrugged. 'Don't really need one, for London.'

'What about when you go home to see your family?'

'Train and taxi.'

'So on a bright spring day, you never get up and decide to go to the seaside?'

'No. But if I wanted to, there's a reasonable train service from London to Brighton.' She glanced at him. 'Is that what you do on your days off? Go to the seaside?'

He gave her a non-committal murmur; given what she'd

already heard his family say to him, she interpreted that as meaning that he almost never took time off.

As he turned on the ignition, the car was flooded with indie rock. Very loud indie rock.

'Whoops.' He turned the stereo off. 'Sorry. One of my worst habits. Volume.'

She'd half-expected him to listen to classical guitar music. Or maybe that was too painful—a reminder of what he'd lost. 'No worries,' she said. 'And I don't mind if you'd rather have music on when you're driving.'

'Just not at that volume, hmm?' he asked wryly, but switched the stereo on again, this time lowering the volume to something much more bearable.

The journey was quick, and he parked in a side street near the Holborn branch. The feel of the place was very similar to the Charlotte Street café, but Fran was intrigued to see that it had its own identity. Different art on the walls, for starters. But the staff were just as warm and friendly as they were at Charlotte Street, and Amy—the head barista—seemed pleased to put a face to the voice from the previous day.

Islington was next, and then Docklands; again, Fran noticed that there wasn't a uniform style to the cafés. 'If you're going to franchise the business,' she said to Gio on their way back to Charlotte Street, 'shouldn't the cafés all look the same?'

'Yes and no,' Gio said. 'I suppose there needs to be some kind of corporate identity. A logo or what have you. But I don't want them to be identikit. I want each café to fit in with its surroundings and suit the clientele in the area. Which means they're different.' He lifted one shoulder. 'I want to keep it *personal*. And sell bakery goods produced locally, to local recipes where possible—so if we expand further afield that would mean Banbury cakes in Oxfordshire, parkin in Yorkshire, Bakewell pudding in Derbyshire and that sort of thing. We'll sell the best coffee and the best regional goodies.' He frowned. 'So I suppose that's an argument against franchising.'

'But if you go the other route and open more branches, you're not going to have time to do a shift in every one, every single week, to get feedback from your customers and staff. Especially if some of them are outside London,' she pointed out. 'With four, you can do it. With five, it's going to be a struggle. With ten—no chance.'

He sighed. 'I'm doing the wrong thing. I shouldn't be looking at franchising—I should be inventing a time machine, so I can make the time to visit all the branches myself.'

'What was it your Italian grandmother says about trusting people?' she asked gently. 'If you expand, Gio, you're going to have to learn to delegate. Trust your managers to do what you do and to give you the feedback. You don't have to do it all yourself.'

'I'm trying to delegate. I'm trusting you to sort the admin side.' He coughed. 'Well. Apart from sitting on your case, earlier.' He parked in a little square just off Charlotte Street.

'Where are we?' Fran asked.

'My parking space, near my flat.' He smiled. 'Told you I lived near the café. It's a ten-minute stroll from my flat to work, tops, which makes life very easy.' He glanced at his watch. 'Are you sure you're still OK for a lesson in lattes?'

'Sure.' Which was when Fran realised that she'd actually been looking forward to it. All day. And even though she'd spent most of the afternoon with Gio, most of the time they'd been with other people.

This would be just the two of them.

Alone.

Strange how that thought made her heart beat a little bit faster.

They arrived back at the Charlotte Street branch just before closing. Once Sally and Ian had left, Gio bolted the door and switched off most of the lights. Then he smiled at Fran. 'Ready?'

'Yup.' She fished her notebook out of her handbag.

'OK. Rule one of milk—it has to be fresh and cold, or it won't froth. It's the proteins in milk that make the foam. And the way we do it is with a steam wand—your goal is to get the froth hole in the wand at the same level as the surface of the milk, so you'll get nice small bubbles throughout the milk instead of huge bubbles at the top.'

'Why do you need small bubbles?'

He smiled. 'I'll show you.' He talked her through how to use the steam nozzle on the machine, starting with half a pitcher of cold milk and gradually working it up so it became warm and frothy. 'This is perfect for a latte. And latte art.'

'Latte art?' Fran asked, mystified.

'It's how you pour the milk in such a way that you make a pretty pattern on the top—the crema comes through in the design. You make a rosetta, swirling the leaves out, and you finish with the stem to pull it all together.' He tapped the jug against the table; then, with what looked like a tiny wobble of the wrist, he swirled the milk on and a flower suddenly appeared in the middle of the foam.

'That's pretty,' she said. 'You make it look very easy— would I be right in saying it's quite difficult?'

'It's advanced baristaing—an extra,' he admitted. 'It's what the coffee tastes like that counts most, not what it looks like. If you've made vile coffee, it doesn't matter how pretty it is— the customer won't want to come back. And then again, some people don't even notice; they add sugar and stir, and your rosetta's gone so you might just as well not have bothered. But it sometimes makes the customer's day when they see a heart or an apple or a flower or a rosetta on the top of their coffee.'

'Latte art.' He had to be teasing her.

He spread his hands. 'If you don't believe me, look on the internet. There are pages and pages of photos of latte art.'

She still wasn't sure if he was teasing her or not. But she liked the way his eyes crinkled at the corners when he smiled, the way his eyes glittered.

'OK. Remember how to make an espresso?' he asked. 'Normally, you'd froth the milk at the same time, but as it's your first time we'll do the milk second.'

'Grind, dose, tamp, fit the filter and pour,' she said.

He nodded, looking pleased. 'Go for it.'

To her relief, the espresso came out well.

'Now to steam and froth the milk.' He guided her through the process, just as he had when he'd taught her to make an espresso. When he moved the steam nozzle for her with a clean cloth, his arm brushed against hers, the brief touch of his skin making her temperature sizzle.

This was crazy. She was known for being level-headed at work, good in a crisis. Reliable, calm and efficient. So why did she feel right now as if fireworks were going off inside her head? Why did she want to leave the coffee where it was, forget the milk, twist round in Gio's arms and brush her mouth against his?

Focus, she reminded herself.

'When you turn the pressure down, can you hear the change in the sound of the steam tap?' he asked.

Low and husky—just like Gio's voice. 'Yes.'

'Good. Bring the nozzle up a tiny bit—remember, we're trying to keep the steam coming out almost at the surface of the milk—and let it froth.' He was standing behind her, one arm either side of her, his hands resting on hers to help her keep the jug in the right place. 'When the jug feels hot to the touch, the milk's ready.'

She certainly felt hot right now. Hot and very bothered. Because his hands were strong and capable, and she could smell his clean personal scent, mixed with a citrussy tang which she assumed was shower gel or shampoo. A scent that she found incredibly arousing; she just hoped that Gio couldn't see the way her nipples had tightened under her shirt.

'You're picky.'

'Details are important,' he said. 'My customers expect the best. And I wouldn't produce anything less.'

'And yet your office is untidy. I thought perfectionists were that way about everything,' she said.

He laughed, the smile-lines around his mouth deepening. 'I'm a perfectionist about *some* things.'

For a brief moment—before she managed to suppress it—the idea flickered through her brain. What else would Gio be a perfectionist about? Kissing? Making lo—

They were making *coffee*, she reminded herself. Flirting and what have you was *not* on the agenda.

'What we're looking for is texture. Tiny microbubbles that make the foam and the milk one—so it settles out in the cup, not the jug. It's got a sheen like quicksilver,' Gio told her. 'We're looking for pure silk.'

Silk. Like his skin. Like his voice.

Oh, lord. She was going to drop the wretched jug in a minute.

'OK. This'll do nicely. Now, what I showed you was free-pouring—but that's quite time-sensitive, and you need to build up to that. For now, we'll spoon.'

Her mouth went dry at the thought. 'Spoon.'

'Spoon the froth from the jug.'

Oh-h-h. The picture that had flickered into her mind at the word 'spoon' had nothing to do with coffee or cutlery. She was really, really going to have to watch what she said.

'Let the jug rest for a little while, so the foam and milk separate out a bit. Then you scoop the foam out of the jug and on to the surface of the espresso. A little bit for a latte.'

She did as he instructed.

Spoon. She couldn't get that picture out of her head.

The picture of Gio's body wrapped round hers.

Naked.

'Then you hold the froth back in the jug with the spoon and pour the milk on to the coffee. It should go through the foam and lift it up, and mix with the coffee.'

She'd barely heard a word he was saying. Tonight, she'd have to go and research it on the internet, so she could make some notes—and maybe try again tomorrow when it was quiet and preferably when Gio was on a break.

'Like so.' He smiled at her. 'The perfect latte. Try.'

'It doesn't look as pretty as yours.'

'You can cheat a bit—some people spoon a tiny bit of foam on top of the crema and make it into a swirl with the back of a spoon. Or you can use a needle to make patterns, like starbursts or the kind of feathering a pastry chef does with icing,' he said. 'Or cheat even more and use chocolate syrup and a knife. But free-pouring's the proper art.'

'And it takes weeks to learn, you say?'

His eyes lit up. 'Sounds as if you're up for a challenge. I'll teach you how to do it. And if you can do it by the end of your trial period, I'll take you to Fortnum's and buy you the biggest box of chocolates of your choice.'

'And if I can't?'

'Then *you* buy *me* the chocolates.' He moistened his lower lip in a way that made her heart beat just that little bit faster. 'And I should warn you that I'm greedy.'

Fran had a nasty feeling that she could be greedy, too.

And it took every single bit of her self-control to stop her sliding her arms round his neck and jamming her mouth over his.

CHAPTER FIVE

'LATTE art,' Fran said, rolling her eyes, when Gio set the cup down on her desk the following morning. On the top was a heart—with concentric rings round it. 'You're showing off, aren't you?'

He pantomimed surprise. 'You mean, you noticed?'

'Just a tad.' She'd noticed something else, too—the guitar case tucked away in the corner of the office. But she hadn't brought it up in discussion with him. After what he'd told her about the way his music studies had crashed and burned, she had a feeling that he was sensitive about it. She wasn't going to push him to talk about it unless he was ready. 'Thank you for the coffee. Now, if you want me to sort out these figures for you, go away and leave me in peace.'

'Your wish is my command.' He gave her a deep bow, followed by one of the knee-buckling smiles. 'I'll come and get you when the cake lady's here.'

'Cheers.' She smiled back, then got to work with the spreadsheet.

Gio leaned through the office doorway at the perfect moment: just when Fran had finished the stats. She printed them off and waved them at him.

'I'll look at them afterwards,' Gio promised. 'But come and taste the goodies first.'

He introduced Fran to Ingrid, the baker, who talked them through the samples she'd brought. 'And I'm leaving before you all start trying them,' she said. 'There's nothing worse than doing a taste-test and not being able to give an honest opinion because you don't want to hurt someone's feelings. Give me a call, Gio, when you're ready. Nice to meet you, Fran, Sally and Ian.' She shook their hands, smiled and left.

'Perfect timing,' Sally said. 'The morning rush is over, the lunchtime one won't start for another twenty minutes—and we have chocolate cake. Oh, *yessss*. Those brownies are mine, all mine.'

Gio produced a knife and cut both the brownies into two. 'No, they're not. We're splitting them all four ways. Except for the Amaretti, which are all mine.'

'In your *dreams*,' Fran said, scooping one of them and taking a nibble. 'Oh, wow. Intense.'

'Intense, good or intense, bad?' Gio asked.

'Definitely bad,' she fibbed. 'Let me save you the trouble of eat—' She didn't get to finish the sentence, because Gio simply leaned over and took a bite from the Amaretti she was holding.

The feel of his mouth against her fingers sent a shiver of pure desire down her spine. Bad. Very bad. This was meant to be a tasting session. And they were tasting food, not each other. They were in the middle of his coffee shop, for goodness' sake! Sally and Ian were there, and a customer could walk in at any moment.

This was even worse than their coffee-making lessons. Because this time it wasn't just the two of them. She really, *really* had to get a grip.

'Mmm. Perfect,' he said huskily.

He was talking about the biscuit. Not about her skin, she reminded herself sharply.

'These flapjacks are good, too,' Ian said.

'*Brownies*. Oh-h-h. I need more brownies,' Sally said, clutching her heart dramatically. 'Save me. Give me brownies.'

'Too late, Sal. You'll have to make do with carrot cake.' Gio handed her a piece wrapped in a paper napkin.

Lord, he had a beautiful mouth. Fran knew she should just stop watching him eat. The last thing she wanted was for her new boss to think she had the hots for him. And she could definitely do without Sally and Ian noticing the state she was in and teasing her about it.

When the samples had been reduced to crumbs, they looked at each other. 'Well?' Gio said.

'They're good,' Ian said. 'Better than our current range.'

'And this is Fitzrovia,' Sally said. 'Organic food is definitely on the up in this area.'

Gio nodded. 'Our coffee's ethically farmed, so organic cakes and pastries fit with the ethos of Giovanni's. Especially as these have no packaging. Eco-friendly and caring—that's good. Fran?'

'I checked out the local competition on the net. If we sell organic, that gives us differentiation from the others,' she said. 'Is our coffee organic?'

'No, but you can talk to the supplier and see what they can offer us, so it's a possible option—in the same way that we can do decaf on request,' Gio said. 'Do the figures stack up?'

She nodded. 'We'll need to put the prices up a little bit, because the wholesale price is higher than the non-organic cakes. But, as Sally said, our customers are the sort who put ethics above economics.'

Gio smiled. 'Good. We'll trial fifty-fifty to start with, see how it goes. Starting on Monday. Give it a month, see how it's affecting sales. If they're the same, we'll make a whole-sale switch.'

'I think,' Sally said, 'you should ring Ingrid and say we're not sure about the brownies—we need some more for testing. A lot more. A whole trayful—no, make that a whole ovenful.'

Gio ruffled her hair. 'Yeah, yeah, Sal. She'll *really* believe that. Thanks, team. Fran, I need to go over to Docklands. Can you draft me a letter to Ingrid about the trial?'

'Sure.'

'Thanks. See you later.'

She loved the way he trusted her enough to get her to draft the letter, instead of dictating it to her over the phone when he got to Docklands. Although she'd adored her job at the voiceover studio, this job was turning out to be a real buzz, too. He'd listened to what she had to say about franchising, too. What she thought *counted*.

Though it wasn't just that, she thought as she headed back to the office. It was working with Gio that gave her the buzz. Because there was definite chemistry there—the way he'd eaten that Amaretti from her fingers...

But she needed to keep her feet on the ground. It was stupid even to contemplate any sort of relationship other than a working one with Gio. She already knew he didn't do rela-tionships and he was at a place in his life where he didn't really know what he wanted. Yes, he flirted with her and teased her, but he did that with just about everyone—so she'd better not start getting any ideas.

She drafted the letter for Gio's approval and was just about to ring through the order to the supplier when she was aware that someone had walked into the office. She looked up, and recognised the woman from the photo on the computer.

'Hello. You're Gio's mum, aren't you?'

Mrs Mazetti looked a bit thrown. 'How did you know?'

'Apart from the fact that he has your eyes, you mean?' Fran smiled, and flicked through the computer screens to show her the wallpaper. 'This is how I know.'

'Oh!' She looked pleased. 'I didn't know he had a photo here.'

'Do have a seat, Mrs Mazetti. Can I get you a coffee and a pastry or something?'

'No, but thank you for offering. Is Gio around?'

Fran shook her head. 'Sorry, he's at the Docklands branch this afternoon—do you want me to ring through to him and get him to come back?'

'No, no, it's fine.' Mrs Mazetti flapped a dismissive hand. 'I know I shouldn't really bother him when he's working. He hates being disturbed when he's busy.'

'Is it anything I can help with? I'm Fran, his office manager, by the way.'

'Angela Mazetti.' She took Fran's outstretched hand and shook it. 'I thought you might be Francesca.'

It was Fran's turn to be thrown. 'Why? Has he said something about me?'

Angela rolled her eyes. 'Of course not. I'm his mother. Giovanni never tells me *anything*.'

'Ah. Marco was your mole?' Fran guessed.

Angela laughed. 'Oh, dear. Was it that obvious?'

Fran laughed back. 'Gio says you're all ganging up on him and trying to get him to settle down, Mrs Mazetti.'

'Call me Angela,' the elder woman said. She sighed. 'We don't gang up on him really. We just worry about him. When you have a son of your own, you'll know exactly what I mean.'

Having a child wasn't on her list of immediate plans, Fran thought, but she tried her best to look sympathetic.

'So are you settling in OK?' Angela asked.

Fran nodded. 'Everyone's been really nice. And Gio's lovely to work with.'

'Good.' Angela gave her a speculative look. 'So you're just colleagues.'

'Yes. And he's an excellent boss. He expects a lot from his staff, but he's fair and he's honest—so everyone's happy to make the extra effort.'

'Hmm.' Angela stood up again. 'Well, I can see you're busy, so I won't keep you. It was nice to meet you, Fran.'

'Shall I tell Gio you dropped in?' Fran asked.

Angela raised an eyebrow. 'I could say that I was just passing...but he'd never believe that.' She gave Fran a rueful smile. 'And, from the look on your face, neither do you.'

'Well, of course you'd want to check me out. Make sure I'm not some kind of bombshell man-eater who isn't going to treat your son properly—or some kind of incompetent airhead who's going to cause him extra work to sort out the mess she's made so he'll be under even more stress.'

Angela laughed. 'Consider me suitably reassured. Welcome to Giovanni's, Fran. And if you're ever at a loose end on a Sunday, you're always welcome to come to lunch at our place. Don't ever feel you're intruding, because we normally have a houseful and there's always room for one more.'

'That's very kind of you.' The sheer warmth of the invitation made Fran's throat feel tight. But if she burst into tears she'd have to explain, and she didn't want Gio's mum to think she was a flake. 'Thank you.' Please, please don't let Angela Mazetti hear the wobble in her voice.

'*Ciao,*' Angela said, the corners of her eyes crinkling, and left the office.

Fran was too busy for the rest of the afternoon to notice the time but, exactly as the previous day, she was aware of the precise moment that Gio returned: just about at closing time. She finished what she was doing and saved the file, then walked into the coffee shop. 'Hi.'

Gio turned to face her. 'Hi. Had a good afternoon?'

'Fine, thanks. I've done the letters for you, a bit of research on that project you asked about, and all the orders are sorted for tomorrow and Monday.'

'Brilliant. It's so good to know I don't have to stop what I'm doing and sort it all out myself. And having this extra time… You know, maybe my family's right and I do work too hard.'

Did that mean he wanted to skip the barista training this evening? The sudden swoop of disappointment in her stomach made Fran realise just how much she'd been looking forward to it.

But then he asked, 'Do you still have time to stay and learn about cappuccinos?'

Pleasure fizzed through her—a feeling she tried to damp down, because she knew it wasn't just the fact she was learning something new. It was because she'd be close to Gio. 'Sure,' she said, aiming for insouciance.

Gio was cross with himself for feeling so pleased that she was staying late again. And crosser still when he realised it was more than just pleasure at a new employee showing commitment to the café chain.

The real reason it made him happy was because he was going to be close to Fran.

When she'd hugged him yesterday, he hadn't been able to stop himself hugging her back. And it had taken all his strength of will to let her go again.

This was bad. Really bad. Because now was just about the worst possible time to start a relationship, when he was thinking of taking the business up another gear and he had no free time. And Francesca Marsden was just about the worst possible person he could think of to have a relationship with, because she was his new office manager and he was going to need her help in the business. He couldn't afford to lose someone who'd already shown initiative and drive and an ability to second-guess him.

He locked up, then motioned her towards the coffee machines. 'Same as yesterday with the milk and the espresso, but this time you're making cappuccino. That's a third coffee, a third milk and a third froth. You'll need to rock the jug a bit as you pour—or you can spoon the froth on top if you find it easier.'

He watched her as she worked. When she was concentrating, he noticed, she caught the tip of her tongue between her teeth. And it made him want to lean forward and touch the tip of his tongue to hers. Kiss her. Mould her body against his. Feel the weight of her breasts as he cupped them.

He swallowed hard, just as she looked up and slid the cup in front of him. 'Is this OK?'

'Looks good.' He tasted it. 'You need a touch less milk and a touch more froth, but for a first attempt it's excellent.'

'Thank you.'

'When you've done your food hygiene course, you can practise on some customers. In the quiet spots of the day, that is; I wouldn't expect you to handle the morning, lunchtime or mid-afternoon rush, first off.' He smiled at her. 'And now I ought to let you go home.' He didn't want her to go—but on the other hand, it was probably better for his rapidly un-ravelling self-control that she did. 'Your family's going to be beating my door down and yelling at me for making you work too hard.'

'I doubt it. They know I'm a big girl and I can look after myself.'

She'd clearly aimed for a flippant note, but he could hear the underlying hurt. What was wrong? He fished in the tub on the counter, drew out a chocolate dipper and handed it to her. 'Spill the beans.'

'I don't know what you mean.'

'Yes, you do. You're the eldest of four, but you've hardly mentioned a word about your family. Whereas mine are always around—if not in person, then on the phone or texting or emailing.' She'd met more than one of them, too. 'Sally said my mum dropped by this afternoon. Gave you the third degree, did she?'

'She was lovely.'

'Yeah. She's bossy and she's interfering and she drives me absolutely bananas,' he said with a grin, 'but I still wouldn't change her for anything. I *knew* she'd come and check you out. I bet she'd been skulking in the street, wearing dark glasses and hiding behind bay trees in big pots, until she saw me leave and knew the coast was clear to come and vet you.'

Fran laughed, but he could still see the sadness in her eyes. 'Tell me about your family,' he said softly.

She took a deep breath. 'I'm adopted. My parents didn't think they could have children. So they adopted me…and then the twins came along. And then Suzy.'

He reached out slid his hand over hers. Squeezed it. 'Hey.

There's nothing wrong with being adopted. It just proves your parents really wanted you to live with them. They chose you.'

She swallowed hard. 'That's what they said, when they told me the truth about my parentage. That I'm special because they chose me.'

'And then being able to have more children was a bonus for them. An unexpected bonus.'

'Maybe. But I'm not like Suzy or Dominic or Ted. I…' She struggled to pull her hand away. 'Oh, just ignore me. I'm being wet.'

'No.' He refused to let her hand go. 'Have you told your parents how you feel?'

She shook her head. 'I don't want to hurt them or make them feel I don't appreciate what they've done for me over all the years. But I know I'm a disappointment to them. The others were all good at sport and exams, and I'm not.'

'But look at what you *are* good at,' Gio said. 'You've got tons of common sense—something a lot of highly academic people don't have. You're good with people. And you're scarily organised. I'm willing to bet you anything you choose that they don't see you as a disappointment.' He paused. 'Something else Nonna says. You never treat your children the same, because they're all different. But you treat them equally. And you love them the same amount—just for different things.'

She gave him a smile that didn't quite reach her eyes. 'Maybe.'

'Definitely.' How on earth could Fran not fit in to her family? She'd been here less than a week and already she was part of the team. He'd noticed a couple of times this afternoon that the Docklands team had been halfway to dialling Fran to ask for help sorting out a problem before remembering that he was there on the spot.

But maybe being adopted gave you a different perspective. Fran's birth parents had given her away, so no doubt there was a part of her that would always worry her new family wouldn't want her, either. That there was something about her that made her unlovable.

'Have you ever tried finding your birth parents?' he asked quietly.

She shook her head. 'I've never wanted to. I'm sure they had good reasons at the time for not keeping me.'

And if she managed to trace them and they didn't want to know her, Gio knew that a second rejection would shatter her trust in people completely.

Right now, Fran needed security—something Gio knew he couldn't give her in a relationship, given that he didn't know what he wanted from life right now. But he could definitely make her feel part of Giovanni's.

'It's good that you're not judging them too harshly. Not bitter about it.'

'There's no point. Being bitter isn't going to change anything or make things better.' She shrugged. 'Besides, Mum and Dad gave me a stable home.'

She hadn't mentioned love, Gio noticed, something he'd always taken for granted in a large and noisy family where you got hugged and kissed every day and told how special you were. And even though the demonstrativeness had been excruciatingly embarrassing during his teens—especially when his parents insisted on showing all his baby photos to any girl he brought home—he'd always known he fitted in, that he was part of the family.

'Your family's proud of you,' he said softly. 'Maybe they're not good at telling you—maybe they're English and reserved instead of Italian and over-demonstrative like my lot. But my guess is they're proud of you. And they're going to get even prouder when Giovanni's expands and your parents realise that their daughter is the number two in the company.' He squeezed her hand again, and this time let it go. 'Want my advice? Go home, ring them and tell them you love them.'

'I might just do that.'

'No "mights". Do it. It'll make you feel better.' He smiled at her. 'Go home. I'm not going to make you stay really late on a Friday night.' Even though what he wanted to do with her would take the rest of the weekend, let alone the night. Because he was going to be sensible about this. 'I'll see you on Monday, OK?'

'Sure. Have a nice weekend.'

He laughed. 'You'll never know how glad I am that you didn't say, "Giovanni Mazetti, don't you work *too* hard"…'

CHAPTER SIX

'Morning, Fran. How was your weekend?' Gio asked as she walked into the coffee shop on the Monday morning.

'Fine, thanks. Yours?'

'Fine.'

She'd just sat down when he brought a latte in to her. This time, there was the shape of an apple floating on the crema. 'You're definitely showing off. Flowers, hearts, apples...'

'Just you wait. Tomorrow I'll do you an ammonite,' he said with a grin.

She scoffed, 'No *way* can you free-pour an ammonite.'

'I didn't actually say I'd free-pour it. I said I'd do you one.' He looked thoughtful. 'But as challenges go...that's a good one.' He leaned against her desk. 'Did you do what I suggested, on Friday?'

She nodded. 'Thanks for the advice.'

'Don't thank me—it's Nonna's wisdom, not mine. She says you can never tell people too often that you love them. And no doubt, as she's coming over from Milan soon, you'll get to thank her in person.' Gio sighed. 'I have this feeling she'll be "just passing" the café, like Mum was. And when she's finished grilling you, she'll start on me. Telling me that I work too hard, and I need to find myself some *bella ragazza* and settle down and produce a great-grandchild for her to spoil.' He rolled his eyes. 'I'm really hoping that she gets distracted by her newest great-granddaughter. Lorena's absolutely gorgeous.' He pulled his mobile phone from his pocket and flicked through the photographs. 'See?'

For someone who was so adamant that he didn't want babies, Fran thought, Gio had a very soppy look on his face. She'd bet he had a picture of every single child in his family on his mobile phone. Not that she was going to take him to task for being a fraud. 'She's lovely,' she said.

'Nonna will enjoy cuddling her. But then again, it'll probably make her worse. Once she gets started on this settling-down stuff…'

'You can always try distracting her with latte art,' Fran said, laughing and gesturing to her mug.

'I could even draw her a bat with a long nose, to make the point. But she'd only laugh and say I was trying to get her off her favourite subject. Like when is her youngest grandson going to settle down,' he said ruefully.

The week got better and better. Gio switched to etching pictures in her coffee, from the promised ammonite through to a lion with a shaggy mane and a spider in a web, making her laugh. Fran teased him back by making a rosetta in his latte with chocolate syrup and ignoring his demands to see a proper free-poured rosetta—she was still a long way from being ready for that. Though she'd been practising in secret, coached by Sally in return for a promise of half-share in the chocolates Gio had bet her.

Even the food hygiene course on the Thursday wasn't that bad; everything was practical, common sense, and the multiple-choice exam wasn't as scary as the exam papers she remembered from her schooldays. Thirty questions in forty-five minutes—and, as Gio said, she was organised and practical, and most of it was simple common sense. She just had to wait a fortnight for the results. A fortnight that just sped by so she actually forgot about the wait.

The post hadn't arrived before Fran left for work on the Thursday morning, but Fran came home to find a large envelope on the doormat. An envelope with the logo of the college on it.

Her results.

It had been nearly eight years since she'd taken an exam. And she'd been physically sick afterwards, knowing she'd done badly and furious with herself because the second she'd walked out of the exam room all the knowledge had come flooding back again and she could've answered all the questions after all.

And when she'd opened the envelope containing her results—proof in black and white that she'd messed up her A levels and let everyone down—she'd spent the whole day crying, because she was such a failure. Despite the fact her parents had tried to comfort her and said it didn't matter, she knew she was a disappointment to them. They were academics, living in Oxford: how could they not be disappointed that she'd failed her A levels and wouldn't go on to university?

Would she be a disappointment to Gio, the same way?

On the day of the course, she'd felt she'd done OK. The exam hadn't thrown her.

Now…she wasn't so sure. Not with her track record. And she couldn't bear the idea of Gio losing his faith in her. Of letting him down.

But she wasn't a coward. She took a deep breath and ripped open the envelope. Stared at the piece of paper inside. No, *two* pieces of paper. A letter and a certificate. So she didn't even have to read the letter to know.

She'd passed.

She whooped and did a Snoopy dance on the doormat.

She'd actually *passed*!

Gio's belief in her had been right. She'd come good.

And she needed to tell him. Right now. She grabbed the phone—and then replaced the receiver without dialling. He'd be in the office, she knew; although he was a stickler for sending her home on the dot, he worked until at least half past seven most nights.

Tonight, she was going to take him out to celebrate. And they were going to drink champagne. She locked her front door, took the tube back to Goodge Street and walked down to the café. As she suspected, the closed sign was up and the front of the café was dark, but she could see the faint light from the office in the back of the shop. Gio was still there. Still working.

She banged on the door.

No answer.

She knocked again.

Still no answer.

Third time lucky?

Yes.

The frown on Gio's face dissolved as he saw her and unlocked the door. 'Hi, Fran. What are you doing here?'

'You sent me to learn about and understand the importance of food hygiene and hazards, plus good hygiene practice and controls based upon food safety management systems,' she said. 'So there's something I need to talk to you about.'

'Uh-huh. Come through to the office.' He stood aside, then locked the door behind her again.

She followed him to the office, rummaging in her handbag, then handed him the letter.

He handed it back without unfolding it. 'I don't need to read this.'

'Yes, you do.'

'No, I don't.' He smiled. 'I told you that you'd pass.'

'Gio, it's the first exam I've taken in eight years. Last time I sat in an exam room, I screwed it up. I failed.'

'But this time, you did well. Just as I knew you would.'

His unshakeable confidence in her made her feel warm from the inside out. She smiled wryly and tucked the letter back into her handbag. 'Just for the record: yes, I passed.'

'Well done. You can do the intermediate certificate next, if you want.' He shook his head. 'Actually, no. You're on the management side, so it's probably better if you do the HACCP in Practice course.'

Was he testing her to see if she knew what the acronym stood for? Ha. No sweat. 'Hazard Analysis Critical Control Points,' she said with a grin.

'And you'll pass that one standing on your head because you're organised, practical and sensible. Piece of cake.' He laughed. 'Well, a brownie, maybe—if Sally leaves us any.'

Fran smiled back. Then she noticed that his guitar was out of its case. 'Sorry, was I disturbing you?'

He followed the direction of her gaze, then shrugged. 'I sometimes use it when I'm thinking. Let things work in my subconscious.'

'And you're thinking about the franchise options?'

He nodded.

'Would you play something for me?' she asked on impulse, settling herself on the edge of the desk.

He blinked. 'I don't play for an audience any more.'

'I'm not an audience. I'm your office manager. And I just passed my exam, so I deserve a treat, yes?'

'That,' he said, 'is manipulation worthy of my mother—in fact, it's worthy of my grandmother.'

Maybe. But she had a feeling that Gio had given up his music as a penance for what he believed he'd done wrong. And maybe playing to someone else would help make him see that he'd more than paid his dues. That he could have his music back.

So she simply sat there. Waiting.

He sighed. 'I should warn you, I'm out of practice. Not like I used to be.'

'I've never heard you play before, so I don't have anything to compare it with,' she pointed out.

'Even so.'

But he was wavering. She could see it. 'Just one piece? Something short and simple.'

He was silent for what seemed like a long, long time. To the point where Fran thought maybe she'd pushed him too far.

She was about to slide off the desk, apologise and leave him be, when he picked up the guitar.

The notes rang out, sweet and clear, in the office—a slow, pretty tune that Fran half-recognised. And then he changed it; it was the same tune, but this time it sounded incredibly different, as if it were being played by a Venetian gondolier on a mandolin. Then he switched back to the slow, sweet version.

'Wow,' she said, when he'd finished. 'I've heard that before, but I've got no idea what it's called.'

'"Spanish Ballad".'

'Spanish? That middle bit sounded more Italian than Spanish.'

He shrugged. 'It's a technique called tremolo—and it's used in Spanish music as well as Italian. Tarrega's "Alhambra" is probably the best-known example.'

Not one she knew—at least, not by name. 'You didn't sound rusty to me. I liked it.' She paused. 'Can I be really greedy? More, please?'

He blew out a breath. 'As long as you don't ask me to play "Cavatina". I *loathe* that piece of music. My sisters used to warble it around the house just to annoy me.'

She shook her head. 'I don't mind what you play. Pick something you like.'

He played Bach's 'Air on a G String', and she ended up closing her eyes and letting the music flood through her senses; the sound was so beautiful that it brought her close to tears. She didn't recognise the next two pieces, though the style reminded her of the Mozart piano pieces Suzy used to practise as a teenager; and then Gio launched into a fast, flamenco-sounding piece. It sounded as if there were two people playing different guitars, though she knew that was a crazy idea. She opened her eyes just to check that someone hadn't just appeared out of thin air to accompany him—but, no, it was just Gio.

And he looked as if he were enjoying himself, as if the speed and sudden loud flamenco licks were releasing all the tension that had built up inside him.

'That was incredible,' she said when he'd finished. If this was what he called 'out of practice', he must've been a truly fantastic musician in his late teens. Gio had a real talent for music, she thought; but he'd sacrificed it for the sake of his family.

'That was Albéniz's "Asturias",' he said. 'A bit showy-off.' He grinned. 'But since I'm being a show-off…' He launched into another piece, slightly jazzy.

'I really like that. What is it?'

'"Verano Porteño". It's by an Argentinean composer, Piazzolla.'

The mischievous twinkle was back in his eye, Fran noticed with pleasure. Music definitely brought out the best in Gio. 'Should I have heard of him?'

'Probably not—unless you dance the tango.'

She laughed. 'Not with my two left feet.'

'Dancing a tango's easier than making latte art.' He gave her a speculative look. 'Maybe I'll teach you.'

Being musical and having a good sense of rhythm, Gio would probably be a superb dancer. And the idea of dancing a tango with him—breast to breast and cheek to cheek, their bodies moving as one—sent little ripples of desire down her spine.

'In Argentina, there's a saying that everything may change except the tango…but Piazzolla changed it,' Gio said. 'He fused the old-fashioned style with jazz, to make something called *nuevo tango*.'

Given that saying… 'And it went down badly?' she guessed.

'At the time, yes—though nowadays most people think of him as the Tango King. He ended up living in Italy, where his parents' family came from, in the late nineteen-seventies. Nonna actually saw him play in Rome, and said he was completely amazing.' He smiled wryly. 'I normally only play Piazzolla for Nonna.'

'Then I consider myself honoured,' Fran said. 'What does "Verano Porteño" mean?'

'Summer—well, it's meant to be an evocation of summer in Buenos Aires. It's from his *Four Seasons*,' he said, 'which is sadly not as well known as Vivaldi's.' He played a couple of bars she recognised from 'Spring', then put his guitar back in the case. 'Enough for now.'

'Thank you for playing for me,' she said.

'Well, I guess you earned it. Seeing as you passed your exams.' He smiled. 'And I'm glad you came to tell me.'

'Even though, strictly speaking, it could've waited until tomorrow,' she admitted. 'But you believed in me, Gio. I couldn't wait tell you.' She took a deep breath. 'Actually, what I'd intended to do was drag you off to a bar and buy you a glass of champagne to celebrate.'

'That's very sweet of you.'

At his tone, Fran felt her stomach swoop. Oh, no. Now he'd think she was trying to hit on him. And he was going to be kind about it and refuse very politely.

'But I think champagne is overrated. There's way too much snobbery about a few bubbles in some wine. I'd rather have a good Margaux any day. Or there's this amazing Sicilian red wine Netti found that actually tastes of chocolate. It's fabulous with puddings.' He switched off the computer. 'Have you eaten yet?'

'No.'

'Good. Do you like dim sum?'

She nodded.

'Then how about we swap the champagne for Chinese food?'

'Don't tell me.' She rolled her eyes. 'You know the best Chinese in London, and it's something to do with your family?'

He laughed. 'Yes to the first, no to the second. Actually, there were a couple of things I wanted to run by you.'

'So we might as well multi-task it.' She threw his favourite phrase back at him.

'We want to celebrate your exam. We both need to eat.' He spread his hands. 'And we can talk at the same time, can we not?'

* * *

Jasmine tea really hadn't been the way Fran had intended celebrating, but when they were seated in the restaurant, having chosen a mixture of dishes to share, she realised that this was just about perfect.

'So, what did you want to run by me?' she asked.

'We're just about into week four of your trial. Which is practically a month.' His eyes glittered. 'We said a month's trial, with a week's notice on either side.'

Fran went cold. Her boss had told her about the studio merger over lunch. Was Gio about to tell her that he'd changed his mind about her working with him, over dinner? Was this going to be her week's notice?

Then her rational side kicked in. They were celebrating her exam results. And he wouldn't have suggested having dinner or said that he had some things to run by her if he was about to terminate her contract. 'So we did,' she agreed coolly, and sipped her jasmine tea.

If he noticed that the bowl clattered when she returned it to the saucer, he didn't comment. 'I'm happy with the way things are going. What about you?'

She nodded. 'I'm enjoying the work and I like the staff.'

'So can we consider you a permanent member of the team, now? Don't look so worried,' he added.

'I wasn't worried,' she fibbed.

'Then you'll stay?'

'Yes.'

'Good.'

That was the first hurdle over with. Now for the biggie. Gio decided to wait until they were eating and Fran had filled her bowl with choice morsels.

'There was something else.'

'What?' She paused with the chopsticks held over her bowl.

'You know my grandmother's coming over from Milan at the weekend?'

She nodded.

'It's for our family birthdays.'

She frowned. 'Birth*days*? Sorry, I'm not with you. Are you saying you have an official birthday as well as a normal one—like the Queen?'

He choked. 'Not *quite*. My sisters and I,' he said, doing his best impersonation of the Queen's opening to her Christmas speech, 'well, our birthdays are all within a fortnight of each other. Four family parties in that short a space of time is a bit excessive, even for my family. So we tend to celebrate them all at one really big family party.'

'Makes sense. Though I do hope you celebrate individually, as well.'

'Yes.' Well, the girls did. He hadn't bothered, the last couple of years, though he'd invented dinner out with friends so his parents wouldn't worry about him. 'I was wondering if you're busy, a week on Saturday. If you'd like to come to the party.'

Her eyes widened, but he couldn't quite read her expression: horror or delight?

'Me?' she asked.

Surprise, then. Well, he could work with surprise. 'Yup. I can guarantee the food'll be good.'

'And your birthday is when, exactly?'

He coughed. 'In the next fortnight.'

'That's approximate. I asked for exact.'

'Are you coming to the party?' he asked, trying to evade the question.

'Are you going to tell me when your birthday is?'

He scooped more food into his bowl. 'You're not supposed to answer a question with a question. It's rude.'

She smiled at him. 'Of course, as the office manager, I have access to the personnel records. So if you don't tell me, I can simply go into the system and look it up for myself.'

'That,' Gio said, 'is flagrant abuse under the Data Protection Act, Francesca Marsden. It's *illegal*.'

'I could still do it. Or…I could ask your mother.' Fran was inexorable.

He knew when he was beaten. He leaned back in his chair. 'All right. It's next Wednesday.'

'Thank you.'

He raised an eyebrow. 'I think it's your turn to answer the question.'

'Thank you for the invitation.'

He really couldn't tell if her answer was going to be yes or no, and he was shocked by the way his skin suddenly felt too tight. It really shouldn't matter whether she said yes or no.

But it did.

It mattered a lot.

He wanted her there.

'I'd love to come,' she said softly.

Which was when Gio realised that he'd actually been holding his breath.

Oh, lord. He was already in way too deep.

'What's the dress code?' she asked.

He spread his hands. 'Whatever. It's a party. Wear what you want.'

She rolled her eyes. '*Men*. Do I have to ask your mother?'

'I'm beginning to think,' Gio said, 'that's you're just as

scary as Mum, Nonna and Netti rolled into one.' But she'd said yes, so far.

Would she say yes to the next question?

'There's, um, a bit more.' He took a deep breath. So much for thinking he'd felt tense before. What he was feeling right at that moment was G-force tension—the sort you got on one of those rollercoasters that sent you round a corkscrew spiral and then round a series of loops. 'I love my grandmother.'

Her smile definitely said, *I already know that. Are you going batty or something?*

'And because she lives in Italy, I don't get to see as much of her as I'd like. I speak to her a couple of times a week, but it's not the same as seeing her.'

Fran stopped eating, rested her elbows on the table and propped her chin on her linked hands. 'It's not like you to beat about the bush. What's up?'

There wasn't an easy way to put it. And however he phrased it, it was going to sound wrong. 'You know my family has this thing about wanting me to settle down—especially Nonna?'

'Ye-es.'

She sounded extremely cautious, and Gio just knew she was going to say no. But he asked anyway. 'Would you pretend to be my girlfriend while Nonna's in England?'

CHAPTER SEVEN

'LET me get this straight.' Fran wasn't sure she'd heard him correctly. 'You want me to pretend to be your girlfriend while your grandmother's visiting.'

He nodded. 'No strings. If you say no, that's fine—it won't change anything between us at work.'

'Why on earth do you need a pretend girlfriend?' Gio was gorgeous enough to have women lining up to be the real thing. If they could put up with his working hours and always having second place in his life to Giovanni's, that was. Which was exactly why she'd never have a relationship with Gio for real: she wanted to come first.

'I told you, I'm not looking for a relationship right now. But…' He raked a hand through his hair. 'There isn't an easy way to put this.'

'Try starting at the beginning,' she suggested.

'Just don't get offended by anything I'm about to say. Please.' He sighed. 'My mother doesn't believe you're just my office manager. So she and Netti have been talking to Nonna—who now thinks that you're my secret girlfriend. And when Nonna rang me last night…I don't think I've ever heard her so happy at the idea I've finally found someone and settled down.' He pushed his bowl away. 'Bottom line—I can tell her the truth and make her believe it, but it's going to hurt her terribly. She's only staying for a few weeks. And…' he looked away '…this is going to make me sound either like a sentimental fool or incredibly morbid, but Nonna's not going to be around for ever.'

She knew exactly what he meant. 'And you want to make her happy while you still have the chance.'

He nodded. 'I'm the only one of my generation who isn't settled down. Even Marcie—my youngest sister—is engaged. All my cousins are married, mostly with children or planning them.'

'So all the pressure's on you to follow suit.'

He sighed. 'Yup.'

'This isn't the right thing to do, Gio. If we pretend we're an item while your grandmother's here, what happens when she goes back to Milan?'

'I haven't thought that far ahead,' he admitted. 'We can split up gracefully—it'll be my fault because you can't stand me being a workaholic, or something like that. And then we can get back to normal.' He waved a dismissive hand. 'Look, I'm trying to buy some time. And there isn't much. Nonna's going to be here in two days.'

'I've worked with you for nearly a month. And I've never seen you panic,' Fran said thoughtfully. 'You're panicking now.'

'Because I can't see a way out of this without shattering Nonna's illusions. Hurting her. Which I really, *really*, don't want to do. She's special to me, Fran. She's always been there for me. Listened to me when I wanted to talk about things I couldn't tell my parents.'

She frowned. 'Gio, this is the twenty-first century. It's perfectly OK to be single, you know.'

'Not according to my family.' He drummed his fingers on the table. 'And I've already disappointed them enough.'

Fran guessed immediately what the root of that particular worry was. And why it was so important to him to please his family now. She reached across the table and took his hand. 'Listen to me, Giovanni Mazetti. You're not a disappointment to your family. Look at you: twenty-eight years old, and you've built your dad's business into a chain with the plan to expand it even more. And you were *not* responsible for your dad's heart attack. It could have happened any time—even if he'd been sitting down relaxing at home that evening, it could still have happened.'

Gio didn't look in the slightest bit convinced.

'Gio, you went to the concert because that was the right thing for you to do at the time—if you hadn't gone, you'd have disappointed your teacher and your family because you hadn't tried, and you'd have spent the rest of your life wondering if you were good enough.'

He lifted a shoulder in a half-shrug.

She squeezed his hand. 'I mean it, Gio. It was the right thing to do, to go. And you *were* good enough. You could've made a career in music, if you'd wanted to. But you gave it up for your family. You put their needs before your own. So no way have you disappointed them. If anything, they probably feel guilty that you gave up your music for them— and I bet they think you've sacrificed your personal life, as well as your dreams, to run the business.'

Gio was silent.

'It's true,' she said gently. 'That's why they fuss about you so much. They love you and they worry about you and they want the best for you. So don't be so hard on yourself.'

'Hmm.' He looked her straight in the eye. 'So was that a yes or a no?'

'Yes or no to what?' a voice enquired next to them.

Gio looked up and groaned. 'I don't *believe* this! Why is it, everywhere I go, I run into one of my family?'

'Because we're on a mission to take over London and call it Mazettiville,' the man said with a grin. 'Imagine how many of us there'll be in our children's generation. Or our grand-children's. Or our great-grandchildren's.'

'That's too scary to think about.' Gio rolled his eyes. 'Fran, this is my cousin Ricardo—Netti's eldest son. Everyone calls him Ric. Ric, this is Fran.'

'Pleased to meet you, Fran.' Ric eyed their joined hands. 'Hmm. I'd heard the rumour. I thought your mum was just hoping a bit too hard. But obviously the family grapevine was right, this time.'

'Oh, for pity's sake…' Gio began.

Fran laughed. 'So much for trying to keep things quiet. Pleased to meet you, too, Ric. And, yes, I'm Gio's girlfriend.'

Gio gave her a grateful look. 'As well as my office manager. But relationships at work are a seriously bad idea, so we were trying to keep it to ourselves.'

'You're on a losing streak there, because your mother has spies all over London. Not to mention Nonna's network,' Ric said, laughing. 'So does this mean you're going to announce your engagement at the party?'

'*Engagement?*' Gio looked utterly stunned. He dragged in a breath. '*Porca miseria*, Ric! You'll have me married with twins next.'

'Nothing wrong with being married with twins,' Ric returned equably. 'In case he hasn't told you, Fran, I have twin boys. Patrizio and Oliviero. They were three last month.'

'I have twin brothers,' she said. 'They're two years younger than I am.'

'So twins run in your family, too?' He smiled at Fran. 'I should warn you—there are rather a lot of us. Though no doubt you'll be meeting us all next weekend at the party.'

'So Gio tells me.' She smiled back. 'And you've escaped tonight for a romantic meal with your wife?'

He nodded. 'It's our wedding anniversary.'

'I did send you a card,' Gio said, lifting one hand to forestall a protest.

'And flowers. Which Alison really appreciated.'

'I most certainly did.' A woman joined them and ruffled his hair. 'Thank you, sweetheart. Hello, you must be Fran.'

'Oh, man. Can't I have a romantic meal in peace without my cousins coming over to interfere?' Gio asked plaintively.

'Not when it's the first girlfriend we've heard of in five years. Of course we want to check her out,' Alison said with a grin. 'Fran, it's so nice to meet you. I've already heard a lot about you.'

'From Angela?' Fran guessed.

'Yes.' Alison smiled. 'The family network can seem a bit overpowering at first—but don't worry, you'll soon get used to it. They only do it because they love each other. Gio's primed you about the party?'

Fran nodded. 'Except the dress code—which he said is "whatever".'

'Men!' Alison rolled her eyes. 'The men try and get away with looking as casual as they can, but the women go dressy. Definitely high heels—oh, and you can make your man buy you a *seriously* expensive bag to go with your outfit.'

Ric groaned. 'I take it that was a hint to me, too?'

'Oh, honey. How *sweet* of you to offer,' Alison teased. 'I'll call Bella and we'll go shopping tomorrow. Gio's middle sister is a handbag fiend,' she confided to Fran.

Gio gently disentangled his hand from Fran's and covered his face. 'I can't cope with you lot. I think I'm going to run away.'

'No, you're not,' Ric said. 'We know exactly where to find you. You'll be in the Charlotte Street café at six o'clock tomorrow morning.'

'Seven, actually,' Gio corrected, lifting his head and looking his cousin in the eye. 'Stop stirring.'

'As late as *seven*?' Ric pantomimed amazement. 'Fran, you've just earned yourself a zillion brownie points with Angela. And…' Ric glanced at his watch. 'Yep. You've got him out of the office a good hour earlier than usual. Make that two zillion points.'

'Don't you dare report this,' Gio said.

'Too late,' Alison told him with a wink. 'I've already texted Jude. But we'll leave you in peace now.'

'In peace? Chance would be a fine thing,' Gio grumbled, but he smiled.

'Happy anniversary,' Fran said.

'Thanks.' Alison tucked her arm through Ric's. 'Now stop annoying your poor cousin and let him have his romantic dinner out. Which is what we're supposed to be doing, too,' she reminded her husband. 'See you later, Fran—Gio.'

'I'm *so* sorry about my family,' Gio said when his cousins had returned to their own table. 'They just…take over. They'll be impossible at the party. You won't get a second's peace.' He shook his head. 'OK. This is what we do. I'll tell a white lie on the night and say you weren't able to come because you have a migraine.'

Fran smiled. 'It won't alter a thing. They'll all drop in to Charlotte Street, the same way your mum did, to check me out. One after another. It's probably easier to get it all over with in one go.'

'Are you sure about this?' Gio asked.

'I just told your cousins I was your girlfriend,' she pointed out. 'So it's a bit too late to back out, now.'

'I could kiss you,' Gio said, his tone heartfelt.

She had to drag her gaze away from his mouth. Because it was all too easy to imagine what it would feel like if Gio kissed her. His lips would be warm and sweet and teasing, coaxing a response from her until heat flared between them.

Until they couldn't stand any more barriers between them and had to be skin to skin.

The ultimate in closeness.

His body sliding into hers.

Oh, lord. She was going to start hyperventilating in a minute.

'Have I told you lately that you're wonderful?' he asked.

'No.'

'Well, you are. You have no idea how much I appreciate this.'

'Just as long as nobody gets hurt,' she warned.

'They won't. OK, we're not telling the truth, but it's for a good reason. It's to stop Nonna getting hurt in the first place.' He topped up their jasmine tea and lifted his bowl. 'Well, here's to us.'

'To us,' she echoed.

On Friday morning, while Gio was at the coffee supplier's, Fran intended to make a few phone calls. But Gio's mother beat her to the first one.

By the time she came off the phone, after promising to go over for Sunday lunch, she was beginning to wonder quite what she'd let herself in for. But she wasn't going to renege on her promise to help him. It didn't take her long to sort out the rest of the arrangements. And, best of all, absolutely everyone agreed to be sworn to secrecy.

This, she thought, was going to be Gio's best birthday in years.

Gio picked her up on Sunday morning at eleven. 'Are you sure you're up to this, Fran? I'll do my best to protect you, but I think you're in for a grilling.'

'Relax. I've already met your mum.' And plotted something with her—not that she was going to let Gio know about that yet. That was a delicious secret she was going to keep to herself. 'It's going to be fine.'

Though the butterflies in her stomach were stomping rather than dancing when Gio parked outside his parents' house.

Relax. This isn't for real, she reminded herself. It doesn't matter if they decide you're not good enough for Gio, because it's not as if you're planning to get married. This is just temporary. Acting a part.

And then they were right in the thick of things—in a houseful of people. Gio started on the introductions. 'Fran, you already know my mum. This is my dad, Giovanni Mazetti the elder.'

'Less of this "elder" business,' Giovanni said, giving his son a pained look. 'I'm not a pensioner *yet*.'

'Pleased to meet you, Mr Mazetti,' Fran said politely.

'Giovanni,' he corrected, ignoring her outstretched hand and hugging her warmly. 'It's good to meet you too, *piccolina*.'

'My sisters, Giuditta, Isabella and Marcella—known as Jude, Bella and Marcie,' Gio said, introducing her to the three younger women Fran recognised from the photograph. They, too, hugged her in welcome.

'And my *nonna*, Isabella Mazetti.'

'Let me look at you, child.' Isabella—who was even shorter than Fran, with grey hair tucked into a bun and deep brown eyes—placed her hands on Fran's shoulders and peered up at her. 'So you are the *bella ragazza* who's made my Giovanni so happy. *Bene*,' she pronounced, and hugged Fran.

'It's nice to meet the woman I've heard so much about, Signora Mazetti,' Fran said.

'Call me Nonna. *Everyone* calls me Nonna,' Isabella said. 'Now, come and sit down and tell me all about yourself. Gio, don't just stand there, get the girl a drink.'

Fran didn't get the chance to ask if there was anything she could do to help prepare lunch. Just as Gio had predicted, she was in for a grilling. And by the time Gio appeared with a cup of coffee, Isabella knew just about everything there was to know about her.

'Nonna, *dolcezza*, give Fran a break.' Gio set the mug of coffee on the side, scooped Fran out of the chair and sat in her place, drawing her on to his lap.

For a moment, Fran stiffened; he hadn't warned her he was intending to do that. But then again, Gio's family was incredibly tactile. Whenever one of them talked to you, there would be a hand on your arm, a gesture, a smile, a patted shoulder. And she was meant to be Gio's girlfriend. Of course they'd expect her to sit on his lap.

So she relaxed back against him, resting her head on his shoulder. His arms were wrapped round her waist, holding her close, and she was acutely aware of the warmth of his body. His strength. His clean scent. The steady, even beat of his heart.

And then it hit her.

This was exactly what she wanted.

Being smack in the middle of a big, warm, noisy family.

Accepted as one of them. With a strong, handsome man holding her protectively.

Oh, lord. If she'd known it would be like this, she would never have agreed to this pretend-girlfriend thing. Because right now she was setting herself up for a broken heart. This wasn't for real, and there was no chance it would turn out that way either—Gio had already told her he didn't want to settle down.

As if he sensed the sudden tension in her, his arms tightened round her, a private signal that everything was going to be fine. No doubt he thought she was just a bit worried about whether his family would believe their story; and that was fine by her. Better than him guessing what she was really thinking.

Lunch was a noisy affair, with everyone chattering and laughing, the clink of glass and the tinkling of cutlery against crockery. A typical Italian Sunday lunch, with a steaming tureen of minestrone followed by beef with crispy-edged fluffy roast potatoes, roasted peppers and aubergines, cavalo nero and all the trimmings.

And pudding… 'Oh, wow,' Fran said as she tasted the first mouthful. 'I've never tasted ice cream this good.'

'Nando's special. Reserved only for the family,' Angela told her. 'Hazelnut.'

Served with a pile of tiny strawberries and a splash of wild strawberry liqueur over the top. 'It's fantastic,' Fran said, meaning it.

And the entire table beamed at her.

After lunch, Fran insisted on helping to clear away.

'No, you're a guest—you sit down with Gio,' Marcie said.

'She's not a guest,' Nonna said firmly. 'She's Gio's girlfriend. One of us.'

Fran had to blink away the tears. How easily she'd been accepted among the Mazettis. And it felt really good to be in this family kitchen, with all the women washing up or drying dishes or putting things away or making coffee, chattering away with half-a-dozen different conversations going on at once and everyone laughing and telling little anecdotes about their week—breaking off every so often to look at a photograph on a mobile phone screen and coo over assorted babies and puppies and kittens.

So different from her own, much quieter and more reserved family.

And the weird thing was, Fran thought with a pang, she felt as if she *belonged* here.

She'd marry Gio tomorrow, just for his family.

And the sudden realisation made her dizzy. If he asked her, she'd marry Gio tomorrow.

For himself.

If Gio's family noticed that she'd gone a bit quiet, they clearly assumed that she was a bit overwhelmed by the experience of meeting the Mazettis, because nobody made a comment. They simply included her in the conversation and asked her opinion on things.

They'd just finished clearing away when the doorbell went. A few moments later, Ric and Angela came in with the twins, who were clearly used to the Mazetti way of doing things because they came to everyone for a hug and a kiss—including Fran.

With their mop of curly dark hair and huge brown eyes, they were irresistible; before she knew it, she was sitting in a chair with both children on her lap, cuddling them and telling them a story.

'She's perfect,' Isabella said softly to Gio.

'Sorry, Nonna?'

'Fran. She's perfect. When you look at her, the emptiness disappears from your eyes.'

'My eyes aren't empty.'

'Sweetheart, they have been for years. I know you've been unhappy. That's why you work so hard, to make sure you don't have time to feel.'

Since when had his grandmother known that?

'But she's the one for you—and she'll make you happy,' Isabella said. 'I like her very much.'

'Good,' Gio told her, striving for lightness. But every muscle felt tight with guilt. He was lying to his family about his relationship with Fran. Worse still, he had a suspicion that Nonna was right—that Fran was the one for him. That she was the one who could make him happy, fill the emptiness.

But on her part this was just for show.

And he'd always said he didn't want to settle down.

So much for his promise that nobody would get hurt. Fran was right: this was going to end in tears. But it was much too late to go back now.

CHAPTER EIGHT

'I REALLY like your family,' Fran told Gio on the way home.

'They're a bit intense.'

'Gio, they're so warm and welcoming. They're lovely.'

Which was what his family said about her, too. His parents and sisters had grabbed him the same way that Nonna had, to tell him privately that they approved of his choice.

No way could he have hurt them by telling them she was just acting a part.

But maybe she hadn't been acting. The way she'd read stories to Ollie and Pat and cuddled baby Lorena... He'd seen a certain softness in her face. A softness that should have made him want to run as hard and as fast as he could, given that he wasn't ready to settle down and have kids—but instead it had made him feel some weird kind of pull. Made him want something he didn't dare put a name to.

'They adore you, Gio.'

And he adored his family right back. He just didn't want them running his life for him. 'They liked you.'

'Good.'

When he pulled up in the road outside her flat, she asked, 'Would you like to come in for a coffee?'

It was a suggestion he couldn't resist. Particularly as he

hadn't yet seen further into her flat than her front door. Her home would tell him a lot about her, he was sure. And he wanted to know more—a lot more—about the things she never talked about at work. Personal stuff. What made Fran Marsden tick?

'Thanks. I'd love a coffee.'

'It's not going to be like the stuff you serve at the café,' she warned, 'so don't expect it.'

He laughed. 'If you had a café-standard espresso machine at home, I'd be a bit surprised.'

'And my flat's very small.'

'Stop apologising. It doesn't matter how big your home is—only how big your welcome is.'

It was her turn to laugh. 'Why is it I can hear Nonna's voice saying that?'

'Probably because it's one of her favourite phrases,' he admitted.

Fran's ground-floor studio flat was very neat and tidy, as he'd expected. The sofa obviously converted to a bed; there was enough room for a few shelves stacked with books and scattered with framed photographs, a small TV and a micro stereo, and a tiny kitchen in one corner with a bistro table and two chairs next to it. There was a small dragon tree in a white pot on the table.

'It's very nice,' he said.

'But it's still very small,' she said ruefully. 'It was either sharing a house or renting a studio flat.' She wrinkled her nose. 'And I wanted my own space. So I chose this.'

Fran didn't like sharing her space? Given the way she'd fitted in so well with the Mazettis this afternoon, that surprised him. Or maybe not—like him, she was part of a large family where having your own space was a luxury. This would be a bolthole for her. Just like his flat was, for him.

He walked over to the window. 'Nice gardens.'

She nodded. 'I'm really lucky that I'm this side of the building and not on the street side. The gardens are communal so the landlord deals with it all—the nearest I have to a garden of my own is my *dracena*.'

He noticed that she used the Latin name—so, was Fran a gardener at heart? Did she have a secret yearning for a house with a garden of her own?

But if he asked her she'd simply deflect the question. He'd already noticed she was very good at that; she rarely gave anything away about herself. He knew next to nothing about her family, other than that she had twin brothers and a sister and they were all academic.

'Go and sit down.' She motioned towards the sofa. 'I'll make the coffee.'

He sat down and watched her as she switched the kettle on and began shaking grounds into a cafétière. Every moment was efficient, economical. Beautiful to watch. But what shocked him was how much he wanted to go and stand behind her, slide his arms round her waist, hold her close and bury his face in the curve of her neck.

This wasn't supposed to happen.

If he wasn't careful, he'd end up believing their relationship was for real instead of a fiction to keep his family happy.

To stop himself thinking about touching her, he twisted round to look at the shelves behind the sofa. There were several framed photographs propped against the books. 'These are your family?' he asked.

'Yes.'

There was one of them all together, very similar in style to the one he had on his computer screen at work—but he noticed immediately that Fran wasn't in it. 'Where were you?' he asked.

'Behind the camera. Which is where I prefer to be.'

'You're worried about posing for a photograph?' Without giving her the chance to answer, he pulled his mobile phone from his pocket, flicked it into camera mode and took a snap of her. He looked at the screen critically. 'It's perfectly OK. You don't take a bad photograph.'

She rolled her eyes. 'I don't have a phobia about having my picture taken, Gio. I just prefer being behind the lens, not in front of it.'

On the outside, looking in? Or was he reading too much into it? He changed tack. 'Is that what you thought about doing when you were a kid? Being a photographer?'

'No, I'm not that arty.' She shrugged. 'I take reasonable snaps, but I'm not under any illusions that I'm the next David Bailey.'

'So what did you want to do, when you were at school?'

'Can't remember.'

Her back was to him so he couldn't read her expression. He had the feeling that she was fibbing, but he didn't want to push her too hard, so he let it go. Instead, he picked up the group photograph and settled back against the sofa to study it more carefully. 'You've met my family. They're going to grill me about yours—and if I say I don't know, they'll smell a rat. Come and tell me about them,' he invited.

'There's not that much to tell.' She brought the coffee over and handed him a mug. 'Obviously that's my mum and dad—Dad's head of the local middle school and Mum's a geography teacher at the local high school.'

Again, he noticed, she'd given him the least information she could get away with. 'Honestly, getting details out of you is like pulling teeth! I ought to take lessons from Nonna. What are their names?' Gio prompted.

'Carol and Warren.'

They looked pleasant enough. Physically, they were nothing like Fran; they were both tall, and, although Warren's hair was graying, he'd clearly been fair, as had Carol. Her siblings were tall and fair, too. So he could see why Fran, being little and dark-haired, felt the differences so keenly.

'Did you take this in your parents' back garden?'

'Yes.'

It was incredibly neat and tidy; clearly someone in the family loved gardening and took pride in the flowers. Something Fran had had in common with them? But he couldn't think of a way to ask without risking her clamming up on him.

'Tell me about the others,' he invited.

She put her mug on the floor, then pointed to the younger woman in the photograph. 'This is Suzy—she's the baby of the family. She's training to be a dentist.'

Again, the bare minimum of detail. What was Suzy like as a person? If anyone had asked him to describe Marcie, the baby in their family, he would've said she was little and funny and noisy and arty—she worked in a gallery and, although she could barely draw a straight line with a ruler, she had a real eye for colour and detail, and the pieces she bought for herself were already worth at least three times what she'd paid for them.

'Does she get more information out of you than anyone else?' he asked.

She frowned. 'How?'

'By pulling…' He stopped. 'Never mind.' It was a poor joke, and he didn't want to annoy her so that she clammed up again. 'What about the twins?' he asked. They were definitely identical; he couldn't tell them apart.

'This is Ted and this is Dominic.' She pointed them out in

turn. 'Ted's a forensic scientist and Dominic's doing a PhD in history—he'll probably go on to teach at uni because he runs a few tutorials and lectures already.'

Again, very little detail. But one thing he had noted: her family were all academic, with three teachers and two scientists among them, and he already knew Fran felt bad about the fact she'd failed her exams. No wonder she felt so out of place—but he'd just bet her family appreciated her other qualities: the way she was unflappable, dealt with things coolly and calmly and was so neat and organised.

And he told her so.

She scoffed. 'There's really nothing to being organised.'

'There is, when you're trying to juggle six things at once.'

She looked at him. 'Gio Mazetti, are you trying to tell me you haven't sorted out your sisters' birthday presents yet?'

How the hell had she guessed that? He hadn't even discussed it with her. 'I'll get there—' he paused '—unless, that is, you're offering help? Because they're at a difficult age.'

She laughed back. 'Rubbish. There's nothing difficult about twenty-seven, twenty-five or twenty-three.'

'Oh, yes, there is. I have no idea what's trendy and what's completely unfashionable.'

'And you think I do?'

He smiled. 'You have a better idea than I have, anyway. Come shopping with me?'

She gave him a searching look, as if trying to work out if his offer was for real; then clearly she decided to take it at face value, because she said, 'Sure, I'll help you find something.'

'Thanks. I appreciate it.' He finished his drink. 'Nice coffee, by the way.'

'Thank you.'

'In cupping terms, I'd say this has a perfect body.' Just like her. Soft and curvy and incredibly sexy. 'I haven't told you about the cupping, have I?'

Cupping.

Little shivers of desire went all the way down her spine. The way he'd held her on his lap this afternoon, with his hands at her waist—if they'd been alone, how easily his hands could have slid up her ribcage to cup her breasts.

Her mouth went dry. 'Cupping.'

His eyes sparkled with amusement. 'It's the coffee world's equivalent of wine tasting.'

Fran could actually feel the colour flooding into her face. Oh, lord. How embarrassing could she get?

Gio's voice deepened slightly. 'Though there is another definition.' The amusement in his gaze was replaced by sheer heat. 'Fran, if I embarrassed you this afternoon when I pulled you on to my lap like that, I'm sorry.'

She wasn't.

He moistened his lower lip. 'My family is…tactile.'

Yes. And she really wanted him to touch her, right here and now. She could see in his face that he was going to touch her. And when he reached out and stroked her cheek, she couldn't help herself. She turned her face into his palm and pressed a kiss into it. 'It's OK.'

'No, it's not.' She could actually feel his hands trembling. 'Because right now I really need to…' In one swift movement, he'd pulled her on to his lap. Except this time she was sitting facing him. He leaned forward and caught her lower lip between his. Nibbled gently until she opened her mouth and slid her arms round his neck, leaning closer. His hands were pressed flat against the curve of her waist. And then his fingers dipped under the hem of her shirt. She quivered as his finger-tips brushed her skin, moving slowly upwards. And then somehow he'd unsnapped her bra, pushed the material aside and was cupping her breasts.

And it was even better than she'd imagined, a few moments before.

When he broke the kiss to trace the curve of her neck with his mouth, she made a little noise of pleasure.

And Gio stopped.

Stared at her, shock blanching his face.

'I... Fran. I'm sorry. I shouldn't be doing this.'

Before she could protest that it was OK, that she was there all the way with him, he restored order to her clothes and gently moved her off his lap.

'This wasn't... Fran, I don't do relationships. And I respect you too much to sleep with you and push you out of my life.'

Respect. What was it about her that made men want to respect her, be her friend, instead of seducing her? Most of the time it didn't bother her.

Right now, it did.

Especially because it would be all too obvious how aroused she was.

The only thing she could salvage from this was pride. So she made the effort to sound like the cool, efficient office manager she was supposed to be. This girlfriend business was just for show and what had just happened between them was—well, they'd both been under pressure. 'No worries. We'll just pretend it never happened.'

'Thank you.' He stood up. 'I, um—see you tomorrow.'

She nodded. 'And bring your credit card.'

'Credit card?'

'Your sisters' birthday presents. We're going shopping in my lunch hour.'

And the minute he left, she was going to take a very, very cold shower. Get her brain and her body back to normal.

Shopping? More like a military operation, Gio thought when Fran marched him into the third shop in Oxford Street. 'What did you do—scope things out on the net first?'

She gave him a sidelong look. 'Don't tell me you'd rather spend hours wandering around, not really sure what you want or where to find it?'

'Well, no,' he admitted. 'But I don't understand how you knew the perfect presents to get for my sisters when you've only just met them.'

'It's called looking at people. Noticing things,' Fran said. 'Jude likes really understated jewellery. Very classic, very pretty. Her wedding ring's white gold and her watch is chrome, so yellow gold earrings wouldn't really be her style. The white gold ones with pink sapphires are more the kind of thing she'd like.'

Hmm. Fran didn't wear jewellery. Didn't have pierced ears. Would she…?

No. He wasn't supposed to be thinking about jewellery and Francesca Marsden. The fact he'd love to see her wearing nothing but a string of pearls and a sexy smile.

Kissing her yesterday had been a big mistake. Because he wanted to do it all over again. And this time not stop touching her until they were both naked.

And sated.

As if oblivious to what was going through his head, Fran continued, 'Marcie, on the other hand, loves jewellery that makes a statement. She wears silver bangles set with big chunky stones. That triangular pendant set with a turquoise is the sort of thing she'd choose.'

'And Bella?'

She rolled her eyes. 'Don't you listen to anyone unless it's about work?'

Ouch. That was definitely below the belt.

'Angela told us in the Chinese restaurant that Bella's a handbag fiend. Here.' She looked quickly through the display, picked out an evening bag and handed it to Gio. 'She goes out a lot in the evening, so a bag that's big enough to take her phone, credit card, keys and a coin purse is perfect. And this particular designer does seriously cute bags.'

'That little Scottie dog on the front looks just like her new puppy. She probably showed you the latest pictures yesterday.' Gio shook his head in amazement. 'See, this is why I needed you with me. You understand girl stuff. I'd never have thought of this.'

'Don't flannel me. You normally text them at the last minute and ask them for a list of ideas and exactly where to buy them, don't you?' she asked.

Was he that predictable? Or was she just really, really good at reading people? But he loved the way she teased him. 'It means they get what they really want. But this year, I wanted it to be different. So I told them all I was going to get them a surprise.'

'And if I'd refused to come and help you?'

'Then I'd have given them vouchers for a pamper day at their favourite spa,' he admitted. 'But I prefer giving presents to unwrap. Ones that people really like.'

'So all you have to do is notice the details.'

'I do notice details,' he protested as he paid for the bag.

'And because we did all the shopping in about three minutes flat, we have time for lunch.'

Though what he wanted for lunch definitely wasn't on the menu.

She pantomimed horror. 'Tut, tut. Should we not be heading to a branch of Giovanni's?'

'The nearest one's at Charlotte Street. Which means I'd feel forced to go back to the office—and aren't you joining my family's campaign to make me take more time off?'

She laughed, but let him lead her into a nearby café.

'I meant it about noticing details,' Gio said when he brought their tray to their table.

'Such as?'

'You, for example.' The way her mouth was so full and lush and sexy when she'd just been kissed. Not that he was stupid enough to say that out loud. 'Your eyes are the most beautiful colour—the same as the sky at about ten o'clock on an August evening.'

'Flannel.' She looked away.

'Fran?' He reached over and squeezed her hand. 'I apologise for embarrassing you.'

'I'm not embarrassed.'

The bright pink of her cheeks said otherwise. 'I'll take it away from the personal, then,' he said softly 'The only jewellery you wear is a watch, and it's precisely eight minutes fast—which I'd guess is the amount of time it would take to sort out a voiceover studio between slots.'

'Well deduced, Holmes.'

'Why, thank you, Watson,' he teased back.

But he managed to keep the conversation light and impersonal, and didn't try to persuade her to take a longer lunch break when she said it was time to go back to work.

* * *

On Wednesday morning, just as Gio was about to leave his flat, his mobile phone rang.

He checked the display before answering: the Holborn branch. 'Hi, Amy. What's up?'

'You know I was having problems with the steam wand the other day, and you sorted it out? It's gone funny again. I'm trying to get it to work, but could you pop in on your way to Charlotte Street?'

'Yeah, sure. I'll get Sal to open up here. Be with you in a few minutes.'

By the time he'd got to Holborn, the steam wand was working perfectly again.

'I feel really guilty, dragging you out here over nothing,' Amy said. 'But as you're here, I was wondering if we could have a chat about something? There's a writers' group who'd like to meet here on Wednesday evenings and they asked me if we could open late. I know we don't normally do evenings, but I've got a business plan. It'll only take me ten minutes to talk you through…'

More like half an hour, but Gio knew the Charlotte Street branch was safe in Sally's hands—not to mention Fran being in the office if there was a problem elsewhere.

He didn't think anything of it until he was walking down Charlotte Street and noticed something odd about the exterior of the café.

Red balloons tied to the door, he saw as he got nearer.

Balloons that said 'Happy Birthday'.

And when he walked into the café, spread across the back

of the bar was a huge banner that said 'Happy 29th birthday, Gio', surrounded by balloons.

Before he had the chance to take it in, his mother, father and grandmother stepped out of the office, together with Fran. Fran counted them in, and they started singing 'Happy Birthday to You' to him, along with Ian and Sally.

Even the customers joined in.

He'd barely registered that today was his birthday—the post hadn't arrived before he left, and he never really bothered making a fuss over the day anyway.

'I don't know what to say,' he said. 'Balloons?'

'There are twenty-nine—one for every year of your age,' Fran told him with a grin. 'Count them, if you like. Now sit down and I'll make you a coffee.'

His eyes narrowed. 'When did you do all this?' Then the penny dropped. 'That call this morning from Amy—you set it up, didn't you?'

She nodded. 'I needed you out of the way until we'd put up the balloons and banner. But she was going to talk to you about the writing-group thing anyway.'

'You know about that?' At her raised eyebrow, he sighed. 'You did the business plan, didn't you?'

'It was a joint effort with Amy, but, yes,' she admitted.

She made an espresso, then heated the milk. And Gio watched, open-mouthed, as Fran made him a latte and free-poured a perfect rosetta on the top. 'Happy birthday, honey,' she said with a smile.

He stared at the mug, and then at her. 'You made me a rosetta.'

'Mmm. I should've made it a cake and a candle, really. But that would mean using a needle and cocoa, and I thought you might like this a little bit more.' Her eyes glittered with mischief. 'Not to mention a little wager we had—which had a deadline of this Friday, I believe.'

He groaned. 'Oh, no. You've been practising, haven't you?'

'Yup.'

'Which means you win the chocolates.'

She spread her hands. 'Don't blame me. You're the one who set high stakes. Which were, and I quote, "I'll take you to Fortnum's and buy you the biggest box of chocolates of your choice."'

He noticed Sally was beaming, and leaned against the counter. 'You've been giving her coaching, Sal, haven't you?'

'For a half-share in those chocolates? You bet I have!' The barista chuckled. 'Though, I admit, my pupil worked pretty hard.'

'It's cheating. Absolute *cheating*,' Gio said.

'Ah, no. You merely gave me a time limit. You didn't say that I couldn't get anyone else to help me,' Fran reminded him.

'I don't know what to say.' He gestured at the balloons and the banner. 'I really wasn't expecting this.'

Her smile broadened. 'Well, I haven't quite finished yet. In fact, I'm expecting a delivery—' Gio heard the door click open '—about right now.'

CHAPTER NINE

Gio frowned as he saw Ingrid in the doorway. From the look of the baskets on the counter, they'd already had their cake delivery for the day. Why on earth would their baker need to come back a second time?

The answer lay in the large white box she was carrying. 'One special delivery, Fran,' she said, and put the cake between Fran and Gio.

'Thanks, Ingrid.' Fran removed the lid and opened the box to reveal a birthday cake, in the shape of a cup of coffee, covered in what looked like pure chocolate. 'Happy birthday Gio' was written on it in white icing, and there was a rosetta piped underneath his name.

There were no candles; instead, there were tiny indoor sparklers along the top of the cake. And Gio had to swallow the lump in his throat when Fran lit them.

She'd arranged all this—just for him.

At really, really short notice.

'Sparklers?' he asked.

'Well, with twenty-nine candles, we would probably have set the cake on fire and then the café's sprinkler system would've gone off,' Fran teased. 'Besides, these are meant to look like froth on top of the coffee. Smile!'

Before he'd realised her intention, she'd taken a photograph of him next to his sparkler-topped cake.

'Make a wish,' she said as the sparklers burned out. 'And remember to keep it secret or it won't come true.'

A wish. There was one right in the middle of his heart, but he wasn't quite prepared to name it to himself. Not yet.

She produced a knife from behind the counter and a stack of plates and napkins; he cut the cake into slices and Fran handed them round to everyone sitting in the café.

'Is this pure chocolate brownie?' he asked.

'Special order,' Ingrid confirmed.

'For a special guy,' Fran added, then kissed the tips of her fingers, leaned over the counter and dabbed them on the end of his nose. 'Happy birthday, honey.'

Gio caught the slightly misty look in his mother and grandmother's eyes. Fran was playing her part to perfection.

But he had to remember it was just a part—and it was going to stay that way, because he knew she wanted something he just didn't think he was capable of giving her. Security and a happy ever after.

And he wasn't supposed to be letting his heart get involved.

All the same, when everyone had gone and Fran had disappeared into the office to do her usual magic with the admin, he went out to the back and gave her a hug. 'Thank you,' he said. 'I honestly wasn't expecting this.'

'It's your birthday. What kind of girlfriend would I be if I let it pass without comment?' She fished under the desk and brought out a neatly wrapped parcel. 'By the way—happy birthday.'

She'd bought him a present? But… 'You didn't have to do this,' he said. 'The cake was more than enough.'

'Hey. You said I could choose whatever chocolates I liked in Fortnum's. Of course I'm going to buy you a birthday present.' She grinned. 'You'll be spending a lot of money on me. I'm just as greedy as you are—'

Yes, please, he thought.

'—when it comes to chocolate.'

Oh, lord. He needed to get his mind back to real life, not fantasy.

He opened the parcel to discover a black cashmere sweater that felt like a soft caress against his skin. Like her mouth tracing a path down his throat, all warm and sweet and incredibly sexy. 'Fran, this is… I don't know what to say.' He leaned forward to kiss her cheek in thanks, and somehow ended up brushing his mouth against hers. A soft, sweet, gentle kiss that made his body feel lit up from within, like the sparklers she'd put on his birthday cake.

He broke the kiss, and for one crazy moment he almost marched over to the door so he could lock it behind them and then stride back to his desk and kiss her properly, until they were both dizzy with need and took the kiss to its ultimate conclusion. The conclusion maybe it should've reached on Sunday, when they'd been kissing on her sofa. The conclusion he hadn't been able to get out of his head ever since.

And then common sense washed back in.

She'd agreed to help him out by pretending to be his girlfriend, for his family's sake. And he was really going to need her when he expanded the business. So the last thing he should be doing was taking advantage of her. 'Thank you, Fran,' he said quietly, and left the office while his self-control would still let him.

At the end of the day, Fran stayed behind. 'I forgot to tell you something.'

He went cold. 'What?' That she'd found another job? That

she'd changed her mind about accepting a permanent role at Giovanni's? That she had a prior engagement so she couldn't go to the family party on Saturday night?

'Your parents and Nonna would expect me, as your girl-friend, to take you out to dinner tonight, seeing that it's your birthday.'

He shook his head. 'It's OK. You don't have to do that. I'll get a takeaway delivered.'

'No, really. I have to eat. And I have a couple of sugges-tions about the business, so we might as well multi-task it.'

How could he resist? 'Are you saying you'd make me work late on my birthday?'

'Let you, more like,' she teased back. 'I'll meet you outside your place in an hour.'

'So where are we going?'

'Within walking distance.'

He rolled his eyes. 'That's only half an answer.'

'It's the best you're going to get. And the dress code is whatever you like.'

He loved the way she teased him. The way she'd come out of her shell over the last month. He'd wondered if meeting his family would bring out her shy streak even more, but it hadn't—quite the opposite. And he really, really liked this confident, bubbly woman who'd emerged from her slightly too serious exterior. 'So I could wear really loud surfer shorts and the most hideously raggy T-shirt in the world?' he tested.

'If you don't mind people pointing at you and laughing at you, sure.' She gave him the sauciest wink he'd ever seen, and sashayed out of the shop.

He swallowed the disappointment that she hadn't kissed

him goodbye. Well, of course she hadn't. Nobody was here to report back to the Mazetti clan, were they? Besides, they'd agreed to forget about what happened on Sunday.

The problem was, his body refused to forget. He could almost feel the softness of her skin against his fingertips, smell her soft floral scent, feel the texture of her mouth against his.

It drove him crazy.

The more so because he really didn't know how to deal with this.

An hour later, Gio had just come out of the front door when he saw Fran walking towards him.

'What, no surfer shorts?' she teased.

He'd opted for plain black trousers and the light sweater she'd bought him; despite the fact it was summer, it was chilly that evening. 'I thought this might be more appropriate.'

'It suits you.' She ran her hand lightly over the soft cashmere. And even though her palm hadn't actually been in contact with his skin, every nerve end was on red alert.

He was shocked to realise just how much he wanted Fran to touch him. Properly. Skin to skin.

This wasn't meant to happen.

And he was going to have to be very, very careful.

'Though dressed completely in black, with those dark glasses on as well…' She tutted and sucked in a breath. 'You look a bit like a James Bond wannabe.'

'And how do you know I'm *not* James Bond?' he retorted. 'I could be sending out hidden messages in those lattes. Those rosettas could be a special secret-agent code.'

She laughed, and tucked her arm through his. 'So you're

telling me your car is really super-turbocharged, instead of cornering like a tank and doing zero to sixty in about half a day?'

'That's below the belt,' he reprimanded her, laughing. 'So where did you say we were going?'

'I didn't.'

'No clues whatsoever?' he wheedled.

'Nope.'

He gave in, and just enjoyed the experience of walking through London with her, arm in arm. She switched the conversation to favourite movies, and he hadn't really noticed where they were going until she stopped outside Netti's pizzeria.

'Here?' Talk about bearding the lion in its den.

'It's the best pizzeria in London. And it's where you told me you celebrate red-letter days. So as today is your birthday—which I would say is a red-letter day—it seemed appropriate.'

The second he walked through the door, the room seemed to erupt with party poppers—and then there was a rousing chorus of 'Happy Birthday to You'.

As the paper streamers began to settle, he could see that the middle part of the restaurant was full, the usual small tables pulled together to form one enormous long table. All the staff from the four branches of Giovanni's were there, along with his parents, his sisters and their partners, and Nonna. There were two spare places at the far end; one of the chairs had a helium balloon attached, with the number twenty-nine emblazoned on it.

Marco gave him a hug. *'Buon compleanno, cugino mio,'* he said.

Gio was still too surprised for any words to come out.

When Netti emerged from the kitchen to give him a hug and a kiss, he submitted gracefully. And then he let Fran lead him over to his seat.

'I had absolutely no idea you were planning this,' he said. She'd already made a fuss of him that morning. He really hadn't expected her to plan a surprise for the evening, too.

'That was the plan.' She smiled. 'Though I can't take all the credit. It wasn't just me.'

'Fran is a girl after our hearts,' Nonna said, patting Fran's hand. 'It was all her idea. We just helped a bit.'

'Happy birthday, boss.' Amy produced a large envelope and a box at the far end of the table, and it was handed down to him.

He opened the card to discover that all the staff of Giovanni's had signed it. And the present was the new boxed set of remastered CDs by his favourite band—a gift that only someone who noticed things the way Fran did would've thought to buy him. 'I…this is fantastic. I'm a bit lost for words.' Understatement of the year. It had completely thrown him. 'Thank you—all of you. I had absolutely no idea.' He looked at Fran. 'How did you organise this?'

'Same way anyone would organise an office party.' She shrugged. 'It's not a big deal.'

Oh, yes, it was. She'd gone to a lot of trouble to organise this, in an incredibly short space of time and in utter secrecy.

'People think a lot of you, Gio,' she said softly. 'And they want to make a fuss of you, once in a while.'

A fuss he didn't normally let people make.

He couldn't remember the last time he'd spent an evening like this. Although the staff at Giovanni's always had a Christmas party, he usually stayed long enough to be sociable but left early, reasoning that they wouldn't want the boss around to put a dampener on festivities. Tonight, they were definitely letting their hair down—but they were all there because they wanted to celebrate his birthday with him. Share his special day.

Just before coffee was served, he said quietly to Fran, 'This is the best birthday I've had in years. It's been really wonderful. Because of you.'

'My pleasure.'

For a moment, their gazes meshed and held. Was he seeing what he wanted to see, or did that expression in her eyes mean…?

The moment was lost when Marco brought round the coffee.

'And Amaretti for luck,' Nonna added, fishing a box from under the table and handing it to Marco so he could share them out.

'Why for luck?' Fran asked.

'You don't know the story? About three hundred years ago, the cardinal of Milan went to pay a visit to Saronno, a poor town where two lovers worked, but they had little chance of marrying. In honour of the cardinal, they invented the Amaretti biscuit, and wrapped them in pairs to symbolise their love. The cardinal took pity on their plight—he blessed them, allowed them to marry and presided over the wedding feast. And Amaretti biscuits have always been wrapped in pairs, ever since, to remind people of the importance of true love.'

True love.

What Nonna and his family thought was happening between him and Fran.

Guilt throbbed through him. He was lying to them. For

the best of reasons, but still lying to them. And that wasn't who he was.

It wasn't who Fran was, either.

Nonna cleared her throat, and it was clear everyone was expecting him to kiss the girl who'd made it all happen, because they were all looking at him and Fran with the most soppy expression on their faces.

So what else could he do?

He leaned over towards her and touched his mouth to hers. It felt as if the room was full of erupting party-poppers again, a mass of glittering tinsel strands. And when he broke the kiss and opened his eyes, Fran looked as shell-shocked as he felt, with wide eyes and a white face. But all he could focus on was her mouth. A perfect rosebud. Lips he wanted to feel against his again.

Except they weren't alone, and he could hear catcalls and whistles in the background.

Just how long had he been kissing her?

Oh, lord. This was starting to get really complicated.

The next morning, Fran was still shell-shocked. That kiss should've been for show. So why had it felt so real? Why had it felt as if the stars were dancing when Gio's mouth had moved against hers—even more so than the time when he'd kissed her on her sofa?

But she pulled herself together and headed for work as usual.

'It was a good night, last night,' Sally said, handing her a mug. 'Though you look distinctly hung over this morning, Frannikins.'

'I feel it,' Fran said. Not that she'd drunk a huge amount; she just hadn't slept well, the previous night. Hadn't been able to stop thinking about Gio. Hadn't been able to get the fantasies out of her head.

'Gio said to tell you he's in Docklands this morning, but he'll call you later,' Sally added. 'You know, I've never seen him look this happy before, and I've worked with him for five years now. When I realised you two were an item, I was a bit worried at first—relationships at work normally make things a bit sticky. But you've changed him, Fran. Made him relax.'

'Good,' Fran replied, pinning a smile to her face. At first, she'd worried about how her colleagues would react to the idea of a relationship between herself and Gio, but they'd all seemed really positive about it. Now, Fran was more worried about what was going to happen once she and Gio had 'split up', how they'd react to that.

But there was nothing she could do about it right now, so it was pointless fretting about it. She'd deal with it when it happened.

She was busy with a set of figures when there was a knock on the office door. She swivelled round in her chair, and stared in surprise when she saw a man carrying the most beautiful hand-tied bouquet of flowers. 'Fran Marsden?' he asked.

'Er, yes.'

'Sign here, please.'

Flowers? Who on earth would be sending her flowers? But she signed for them and set them on her desk. They were absolutely stunning: sugar-pink roses, white lisianthus, pink freesias and tiny white matricia. She couldn't resist putting her nose into them and inhaling deeply; the scent was beautiful.

She opened the envelope that was tucked into the cellophane, and recognised the handwriting instantly.

Thank you. For everything. Love, Gio.
Love.
Her stomach clenched. Except this wasn't, was it?

When Gio walked into the office, he could see that Fran's eyes were slightly red. The flowers were on her desk, just as he'd hoped—but why did she look as if she'd been crying?

Or maybe… 'Oh, no. I should've checked before I had them delivered. I didn't realise you suffered from hay fever.'

'I don't.'

He leaned against the edge of her desk. 'What's wrong?'

'Nothing.'

'I have three sisters. So I know that "nothing" never really means that, especially when a woman looks as if she's been crying,' he said softly, and gently tilted her chin with one finger so she was facing him. 'What's wrong?' he asked again.

'I'm just being silly. I can't remember the last time someone sent me flowers,' Fran said, 'and I wasn't expecting these.'

'My intention wasn't to upset you,' he said. 'I just wanted to say thank you.'

'And it's appreciated.'

There was the tiniest wobble in her voice. He wanted to pull her into his arms, hold her close and tell her everything was going to be fine, because he was there—because he'd always be there and he'd never let anything hurt her.

But that was the whole problem.

He didn't trust himself not to let her down, the way he'd let his family down all those years before—the way he'd been selfish and stupid enough to put himself first, and they'd nearly lost his father as a result. How could he make her a promise he didn't know he could keep? So instead he kept things light. Ruffled her hair. 'I'm off to Islington. I only popped in while I was passing to see if there was anything you needed here.'

'No, we're fine.'

'And these aren't in lieu of the chocolates, by the way—Sally's already checked. We'll be getting those tomorrow.'

That at least made her smile. Which in turn made him feel less panicky. 'Catch you later,' he said, and left the office before he did something stupid.

Like give in to the urge to scoop her up in his arms, kiss her properly, and carry her to his bed.

CHAPTER TEN

AND then it was Saturday. The day of the party.

Fran rang Angela in the morning to see if she could do anything to help.

'Sweetheart, that's so kind of you to offer. But there's no need—Nonna, the girls and I have everything under control,' Angela said. 'We'll see you tonight. And the idea is that you and Gio have *fun*, OK?'

'OK,' Fran promised.

Which left her with nothing to sort out except what she was going to wear. Although she had a perfectly serviceable little black dress—one she'd worn to functions when she'd worked at the voiceover studio—it didn't feel quite right for the Mazetti party. She wanted something a little dressier. The kind of thing that Gio Mazetti's girlfriend would wear, not his office manager.

She was browsing in the clothes shops in Camden when her eye was caught by a dress. It was a deep cornflower blue, in floaty organza over taffeta. Absolutely nothing like what she'd intended to buy—she'd always thought herself too curvy to wear a strapless dress—but some impulse made her try it on.

She was looking at herself in the mirror and wondering if

she had the nerve to wear it when the sales assistant appeared with a lapis-lazuli necklace.

'I don't normally bother with jewellery,' Fran said, eyeing it dubiously.

'Try it on and see what you think,' the assistant suggested. 'I reckon it matches the dress perfectly. Here—do you want me to do it up for you?'

Ten seconds later, Fran stared at herself in the mirror. The necklace really was the finishing touch, skimming across the middle of her collarbones and throwing the paleness of her skin into relief.

And the bulges she'd feared she'd see weren't visible. Just curves.

'It's perfect. Don't wear anything else, not even a watch,' the assistant said. 'What about shoes?'

'I was thinking black high heels,' Fran said.

'Patent or suede?'

'Suede.'

The assistant nodded. 'Perfect. You're going to blow his mind when he sees you.'

Not when she wasn't his real girlfriend. 'Maybe,' she hedged.

'There's no maybe about it,' the assistant said with a smile. 'That dress was made for you.'

'I was planning to get a little black dress. Something practical that I could dress up or down.'

'You *could*,' the assistant said, 'but, believe me, nothing's going to be as perfect as what you're wearing right now.'

And Fran knew the assistant was right when she opened her front door to Gio and his jaw dropped.

'Wow.' Then he seemed to recover fast and go back to

their usual teasing relationship. 'You scrub up nicely, Francesca Marsden.'

So did he. In dark trousers and a silk shirt, he looked stunning. And very, very touchable.

He reached out and traced a fingertip just below the line of his necklace. The feel of his skin against hers made every nerve end quiver and her pulse speeded up.

'Your dress is the same colour as your eyes. It's fabulous,' he said softly.

And she knew he meant it.

He wasn't paying his pretend girlfriend a compliment in front of his family.

He was telling her this, here and now. In private.

'Not just the dress. *You* look fabulous.' Then he held out his hand. 'We'd better go. The taxi's waiting.'

She locked up and followed him out to the taxi. He held the door open for her—the perfect manners were typical of Gio—and it seemed as if hardly a minute passed before they were there.

'Are you really sure you're up to this?' Gio asked. 'The Mazetti clan is pretty big. It's not too late to back out.'

'I've already met Nonna, your parents and your sisters, your aunt and some of your cousins,' she reminded him. 'It'll be fine.'

'Then let's do it.' He slid his arm round her shoulders, and they walked into the hall together.

He'd said his family was big. But she hadn't expected the place to be so utterly packed. Gio introduced her to person after person; although she was normally good with names, there were so many that she simply lost track.

And she had no idea who was topping up her glass, but the level of champagne never seemed to go down. It would be way too easy to drink too much and make a mistake—say something she shouldn't. She made a mental note to put her glass down and forget about it.

'Francesca, *cara*!' Nonna came over to her, hugged her and kissed both cheeks. 'You look lovely.'

'So do you,' Fran responded politely.

Nonna chuckled. 'Ah, but I don't have that extra sparkle— the look of a young woman in love.'

Maybe Gio's family were seeing what they wanted to see, Fran thought. Or maybe after all these years she'd finally found her hidden talent: acting. Because she wasn't in love with Gio.

Was she?

Before Nonna could say anything else, the band on stage played a fanfare.

Gio groaned. 'Why do we have to do this every year?'

'Because it wouldn't be a birthday party without it, figlio mio,' his father said, laughing and patting his shoulder.

'You know the song,' the singer said into the microphone. 'Four times. Giovanni, Isabella, Giuditta and Marcella.'

The band played the introduction to 'Happy Birthday to You', and then were drowned out by the entire room singing in Italian. *Tanti auguri a te, Tanti auguri a te, Tanti auguri Giovanni, tanti auguri a te!* The song was repeated for Gio's sisters; and finally, there was a rousing set of cheers.

'Your family definitely knows how to party,' Fran said, smiling at Gio when the cheers had died down and the band was playing again.

'Years of practice,' Gio said. 'Let's get some food and escape outside. It's boiling in here.'

Once he'd piled a plate with assorted canapés and dips, they found a quiet corner in the grounds. Gio looked at the bench, then at Fran's dress. 'Some of that varnish is peeling. I don't want it ruining your dress. Better sit on my lap.'

From another man, it would be a cheesy excuse. From Gio, it was practical common sense. So when he set the plate down on the bench beside them, she acquiesced without making a fuss, settling herself on his lap and resting one hand on his shoulder for balance.

The fact that his hand was resting on the curve of her waist really shouldn't be sending these little shivers through her body, she thought. He'd only done it to make sure she didn't accidentally slide off his lap. And she really shouldn't get used to being close to him like this. Close and personal.

Striving to keep her voice normal, she said, 'It's quite an evening.'

'When we were kids, we used to have a bouncy castle and a barbecue in the back garden. But as we grew older and the family's grown bigger, Mum decided to hire a hall and a band.' He sighed. 'To be honest, I'd much rather have a quiet night out somewhere. See a good film or a show. But Mum, Nonna and the girls really enjoy it. They love planning the party and getting dressed up and having an excuse to get everyone together and talk so much that they end up with sore throats the next day.'

'So you put up with it for their sake?' Fran guessed.

'Yeah.' Gio shrugged. 'Just call me Saint Giovanni.'

She gave in to the temptation to stroke his cheek. Freshly shaven. Smooth and soft and sensual. 'You're a good man,' she said.

He turned his head slightly and pressed a kiss into her palm—like the way she'd pressed a kiss into his palm that afternoon when he'd kissed her on her sofa. 'Not really. I let my family down once—at the time when they needed me most. I promised myself I would never do that again.'

'Everyone else forgave you long ago—if they ever blamed you in the first place.' Which, having met his family, she very much doubted. 'Your dad's heart attack wasn't your fault. When are you going to forgive yourself, Gio?'

'I don't know.' He sighed. 'Can we change the subject, please?'

This wasn't the time or the place to push him. 'Sure. What do you want to talk about?'

'Dunno.'

He looked utterly lost, and it made her heart ache. She leaned forward and kissed the tip of his nose.

He looked up at her, his eyes dark, and his hands tightened round her waist. 'Why did you do that?'

She opted for honesty. 'Because you're hurting, Gio, and I want to make you feel better.'

She couldn't help staring at his mouth. Even though he was in a bleak mood, right now, there was still a tiny curve upwards at the corner of his lips. That irrepressible, funny man she'd grown to l—

Whoops. She was getting too much into this role of being Gio's girlfriend. Better remember she was just his office manager, and this was just for show. 'Talk to me,' she said softly. 'Tell me what's wrong.'

He shook his head. 'Just ignore me. I'm in a funny mood.'

She stroked his face again, and her skin tingled at the contact. 'I'm going to quote Nonna back at you. "A problem shared is a problem halved." You helped me when I hit a bad patch. Now you're having a bad patch and it's my turn to help you. So tell me what's put you in that mood. Is it work?'

'No.' He sounded very definite.

'What, then?'

'I don't know. It's just this feeling of something...' He shook his head in obvious frustration. 'Something *missing*, I suppose.

I can't explain it. If I knew what it was, I could do something about it. But there's just this black hole staring at me.'

'Your music?' she guessed.

'No. I still play, for me.'

And he'd played for her, too.

'You could go back to it. You don't have to expand the café chain—it's doing fine as it is. Take a sabbatical,' she suggested. 'Be a musician.'

'How? Busking on street corners?'

She shook her head. 'There's nothing to stop you playing a concert once in a while. An arts centre, a gallery—even in Giovanni's. You're thinking of opening one evening a week in Holborn for the book group. Why not open another evening a week as a classical music night, maybe at Charlotte Street? Play the music you love for people?'

He took a deep breath. 'I don't know. I don't know if I'm good enough, any more.'

'What you played for me was good,' she said. 'OK, so I'm not a music critic and your technique could've been all over the place, for all I know—but none of the notes sounded wrong. I liked it. And there are plenty of people out there who'd like to relax with a decent cup of coffee and one of Ingrid's fabulous cakes and listen to something to help them chill out.'

'Be a musician.' He stared at her, though it was as if he wasn't seeing her. As if he was some place far, far away. 'I don't know, Fran. The more I think about it, the more I'm sure that being a musician wouldn't have been the right life for me. I don't want to be constantly on the road, or doing bits and pieces and trying to scrape a living. I know I wouldn't have had the patience to teach.'

'Are you sure about that? You did a good job of teaching me to make espresso.'

'Which is not the same thing at all as teaching someone who can either sing in tune, but has no sense of rhythm, or can sing with the beat, but is completely tuneless. That's more like nails scraping down a blackboard, and I'm not noble enough to pretend it doesn't matter and gently guide whoever it is into a better technique.' He sighed. 'I just feel I'm looking for something, Fran. Searching. And I don't know what I'm looking for or even where to look.'

'Maybe you'll know when you find it.'

'Maybe. But right now I feel like the most selfish man on earth. I have so many good things in my life. I love my family, I have free rein in my job, I like where I live. So why can't I be satisfied with what I have?'

She held him close. 'I can't answer that. But I do know your family love you, your employees respect you, and you're a good man. Don't be so hard on yourself.'

'Hard on myself? That,' Gio said wryly, 'is most definitely the pot calling the kettle black.'

'But that's not up for discussion.'

He rested his forehead against her temple. 'Now who's being difficult?'

His breath fanned her cheek, and it was, oh, so tempting to turn her head slightly, let her mouth brush against his. Kiss his blues away. But that wouldn't solve anything: that would just put off the problem. Right now, he needed her to keep this light. 'Not me,' she said with a smile. 'Come on. Let's go and dance your blues away.'

After a few minutes of throwing themselves into the music, she was relieved to see that his bleak mood lifted slightly and he was starting to smile again. But somehow they'd moved near to the stage, and the singer had caught sight of them.

'Gio! Come up and play with us, my friend,' he called when the song had finished.

Gio shook his head. 'No, I'm fine in the audience, thanks.'

'Come on,' the singer wheedled. 'You know everyone would love to hear to you play. And sing.'

'I'm fine right here,' Gio repeated.

The singer refused to let it drop, and Gio's face darkened. Considering the conversation they'd just had, for a moment, Fran thought that he was going to walk out.

And then Nonna placed her hand on his arm. 'Gio, *piccolino*, do it for me. Or if you won't do it for me, sing for Francesca,' she said softly.

Tension was coming off him in almost visible waves. But then he nodded. 'All right. I'll do it for Fran.'

He climbed up on the stage, to loud applause and cheers from the audience. 'OK, so it's August and not October, but there's a certain song I want to sing tonight. For Francesca.' He winked at her, as if telling her that it was going to be OK, he wasn't going to make a scene; then he turned and mouthed something to the pianist, who nodded. And Gio made no protest when the guitarist handed him an electric guitar—just checked the tuning.

And then he counted the band in to a soft, jazzy number Fran recognized: 'Moondance.'

It was a song she'd always liked. But hearing Gio sing it somehow gave it something extra. He had the most beautiful voice. So beautiful that it hurt; she found herself wishing that Gio was singing this to her for real, that he wanted to dance with her and call her his love and make love with her.

But his eyes were on her as he sang. And just for a moment she could almost believe that he really was singing this for her. Could imagine what it would be like to run into his arms and dance in a frost-covered garden with him on an October night, the moonlight shining through the almost-bare branches of the trees and turning everything magically silver.

The song ended with him pleading for one more dance with his love. Then he smiled. 'Thank you. That one was for Fran,' he said, and handed the guitar back.

'Oh, come on, Gio—give us another one!' someone called.

'It's my birthday party and you want me to work?' he retorted, laughing. 'Now there's a first. I thought you lot all wanted me to slow down.'

'Just one more song,' someone else pleaded.

'One's enough. Now I'm going to dance with my girl and hand you back to the real singer. Enjoy your evening, everyone.' He stepped down from the stage and joined Fran again.

'I didn't know you could sing that well,' she said. 'That was pretty amazing.'

'Nothing that a thousand pub singers in London don't do every Saturday night,' he said, making a dismissive gesture. 'It's not a big deal. Dance with me?'

The singer had followed Gio's performance with another Van Morrison song, a slow ballad; Fran stepped forward into Gio's arms and swayed with him to the music. If only she could ease his troubles, the way the singer was telling them the love of his life did. But all she could do right now was hold him.

And even when the next song changed tempo and became upbeat again, Fran and Gio remained dancing close, just holding each other and swaying to the beat. Cheek to cheek. So close they could feel each other's heartbeat.

With shock, she realised that this was what she'd been waiting for. To be in Gio's arms. She couldn't pin down the exact moment, but at some point over the last few weeks she'd fallen for Gio—and the whole Mazetti tribe. Which was stupid, because this wasn't for keeps. Their relationship would end when Nonna went back to Italy.

And the knowledge broke her heart.

Gio sensed the sudden tension in Fran, and pulled back slightly so he could see her face. 'OK?' he mouthed.

She nodded and smiled, but although the light was too low to see properly, he could tell the smile didn't reach her eyes. She was definitely upset about something, but she wasn't telling.

Ah, hell.

He wanted to kiss her better.

No. Actually, he just wanted to kiss her again.

And that would complicate matters beyond belief.

He really ought to let her go right now. Put her in a taxi and pay the driver to wait until she was safely indoors. But he couldn't drag himself away from her. So he just wrapped his arms round her again, held her close. Told her silently with his body that he was there, that whatever was wrong he'd do whatever he could to make it right.

Dancing cheek to cheek with her like this meant that he could smell the sweet floral perfume she'd used. Summer roses. Like the candied petals his mother used on a trifle and that he'd always begged for, as a child. So sweet.

His mouth was so close to her ear; he couldn't resist pressing the tiniest kiss to her earlobe. The next thing he knew, his mouth was brushing a trail of kisses along her cheek. Her face turned slightly to meet his. And at last his mouth found hers. A tiny, gentle, questioning touch.

A second's pause.

And then she tilted her head slightly, kissed him back. An equally tiny kiss. The barest touch of her lips against his.

His mouth was tingling. And despite the fact they were in a noisy, crowded hall with people dancing round them, everything seemed to melt away. There was just the two of them. And an overwhelming need to kiss her properly, feel her mouth open beneath his.

He caught her lower lip between his. So soft, so sweet.

His head was telling him that this was a seriously bad idea, but his body wasn't listening. Because this felt as if tiny stars had started to illuminate the black hole in the middle of his heart. The tiniest flickers of light, of hope.

And when her mouth opened beneath his and the tip of her tongue touched his, the lights became brighter. She was warm and soft and her body fitted against his perfectly.

Right here, right now, this was where he belonged. With Fran. No pretence, no act. And the way she was kissing him back made him feel as if he could conquer the world. Walk on air.

'Put the girl down, Gio. There are children present,' Ric teased, slapping him on the back.

Oh, lord. However long had they been kissing? Fran's mouth was slightly red and swollen, her pupils were enormous, and he could feel that her breasts had grown slightly fuller and heavier against him.

He was turned on just as much. And he couldn't get the words of that song out of his head. How much he wanted to make love to her. In a frosted garden. On a swing.

Uh. He couldn't remember the last time he'd fantasised about someone. His life had been too full with work. But Fran…Fran was different.

'Your timing's impeccable, *cugino mio*. Not,' he said ruefully. And Fran's cheeks were crimson. He kissed the tip of her nose. 'Sorry, honey. I got carried away. Give me a second to calm down.' He bent his head slightly and whispered in her ear, 'But please don't move until then, because if you do I think we'll both be extremely embarrassed.'

'I was going to ask you if you were enjoying the party,' Ric said with a smile, 'but I don't think I need to.'

'Tact,' Gio said to Fran with a sigh, 'is not a Mazetti strong point.' He coughed. 'Would you mind not embarrassing my girlfriend?'

'I apologise, Fran.' Ric patted her shoulder. 'For embarrassing you. Though not for embarrassing the birthday boy. *Buon compleanno*, Gio.'

'Thanks, Ric. I think.'

When Gio's cousin left them alone again, Gio stroked Fran's cheek. 'Um. That wasn't supposed to...' He swallowed hard. 'I can't even blame it on too much champagne.' It was just Fran. Her nearness. And how he wanted her.

'Me, too.'

Had he spoken that last bit aloud? Was she saying that she felt the same way?

But right now he didn't trust his judgement.

Right now, he just wanted to get out of here. But the party was a quarter his—he knew he was expected to stay right to the end.

Somehow, they made it through the rest of the evening. If anyone else had noticed them kissing—well, how could they possibly have missed it?—at least they had more tact than Ric and didn't mention it.

They were the last ones in the hall except Nonna, his parents, his sisters and their partners. Just short of a dozen of them: enough to make clearing up easy work.

'Thank you,' Jude said, hugging Fran.

'We know you helped Gio choose our presents. And they're perfect,' Bella said.

Marcie added, 'But most of all, thank you for making our brother human again. I haven't seen him look this happy in years.'

'No pressure, then,' Fran quipped, but inside her heart was heavy. This whole deception had started to avoid Nonna's illusions being shattered. But the way things were going, when she and Gio staged their break-up, an awful lot more people were going to get hurt. His grandmother, his parents and sisters...

And herself.

'Come on, honey. Time to go home,' Gio said, taking her hand.

Once they'd made their goodbyes and climbed into the taxi, Gio let her hand go again.

Well, what had she expected? That kiss earlier—it hadn't been faked, but it hadn't exactly been for real either. A dream that had caught them both up for a while, but now they were back in reality.

They were silent as the taxi took them back to Fran's house, but she was shocked when Gio actually dismissed the taxi. Was he expecting her to invite him in?

As if he could read her mind, he said, 'I just want to see you safely into your flat. And then I'm walking home.'

'But you live ages away.'

He shrugged. 'It's not raining and the fresh air will do me good.'

He followed her into the lobby and she opened her front door. Her tongue felt as if it had stuck to the roof of his mouth, but she managed to get the words out. Even managed to get them to sound light and breezy, as if nothing had happened. 'Would you like to come in for coffee?'

In response, he moved closer and brushed his mouth against hers. 'If I do, we'll both regret it in the morning. Because right now what I want to do is take that beautiful dress off you and carry you to your bed.'

That sexy, husky note in his voice was her undoing. He'd just voiced exactly what she wanted him to do, too.

'Gio.' She reached up to pull his head down to hers. Pressed her body against his, so close that she could actually feel his heartbeat. Hard and fast, like her own.

And he was kissing her back, gently moving her so her back was against the front door. He nudged his thigh between hers, sliding one hand to cup her bottom and bring her even closer to him; she could feel his erection pressing against her, hot and hard.

Fran had never wanted anyone so much in her entire life.

And then he shuddered. Broke the kiss. Disentangled her hands from his hair. Took a step backwards. 'We can't do this. In the morning, I'll feel guilty about taking advantage of you.'

He wouldn't be taking advantage of her. She'd be with him all the way.

'So I'm going to leave now. While I still can.' He closed his eyes. Embarrassment, or because if he looked at her, saw the sheer desire in her expression, his control would splinter?

'I'll see you Monday.' He opened his eyes again, but didn't look at her. 'And thanks for coming to the party with me tonight.' He raised a hand in the tiniest wave goodbye, and left.

He'd done the right thing. The sensible part of her knew that. It would be way too complicated between them at work afterwards if they spent the night making love. Leaving now was the right thing to do—not to mention the complication of this whole fake-girlfriend thing.

So why did it hurt so damned much? she thought as she locked the door behind her. Why did she want to curl up in a ball and cry her eyes out?

CHAPTER ELEVEN

GIO didn't actually see Fran on Monday, because he was visiting a franchise organisation. She was a bit hurt he hadn't asked her to go along with him; but then again, it was probably better if they were apart for a bit. Sensible. It would give them both a chance to cool down and wipe out any lingering awkwardness from Saturday night.

On Tuesday, Gio didn't even call in to the office to see if everything was OK. Which was good, she told herself, because clearly he trusted her to keep everything in the cafés ticking over without supervision. And that stupid longing to hear his voice was just that. Stupid. Teenagery.

Which was even *more* stupid, considering that she was twenty-six and sensible, not fifteen and full of hormones.

All the same, she made serious inroads into the box of chocolates Gio had bought her for winning the bet about making latte art. She needed the sugar rush.

But after work on Tuesday night, things took a dip for the worse. Fran had called in at the supermarket on the way home. But as soon as she pushed her front door open, she could see that she had a problem.

A huge problem.

There was a hole in her ceiling, and bits of artex were scattered everywhere. And from the way her sofa-bed was completely soaked, it looked as if water had come through the ceiling, collected in the gap between the plasterboard and the artex and stretched it out until it burst—sending water cascading straight down. Her carpets were squelchy underfoot, there were stains on the walls from where water had seeped through the gap between the ceiling and the wall, and already she could smell something unpleasant: wet wool, she guessed. Probably the carpet.

For a moment, she just stood staring at the mess, too shocked to move.

And then common sense kicked in. She needed to make a few calls. Starting with the letting agency, to tell them what had happened so they could book someone to come round and start repairing the damage. The insurance company for the damage to her belongings. And work, to say that she'd be in late tomorrow as she had a ton of things to sort out.

Which meant she was going to have to talk to Gio.

Well, this was business and they were both adults. So there was no point in putting it off, was there? She rang his mobile; he sounded slightly absent when he answered, as if she'd interrupted him in the middle of something and he was only paying half attention to the call.

'It's Fran. I'm afraid I won't be in tomorrow—at least, not until late—because I need to sort out a problem.'

Her voice sounded tight and slightly anxious, not her usual cheerful self. Gio, who hadn't really been listening, suddenly snapped to attention. 'What sort of problem?'

'My flat's been flooded. It's a bit of a mess. I just need to sort a few things out.'

She was clearly aiming to sound practical, but the tiny

wobble in her voice told him how upset she really was. Knowing Fran, 'a bit of a mess' was an understatement. And even though he knew it was sensible to keep his distance for a little bit longer and she was perfectly capable of dealing with the problem by herself, he couldn't just stand by and leave her to it. 'I'm coming over.'

'Gio, you really d—'

'I'm on my way *now*,' he cut in. He ended the call, closed the file he was working on, locked the door behind him, collected his car and drove straight to her flat.

Her face was tight with tension when she opened the door to him. Because she didn't want to face him, or…?

Then he glanced over her shoulder and saw the mess.

'*Porca miseria*, Fran! How did this happen? A burst pipe?'

She shook her head. 'The guy above me left the bath running. He was on the phone to someone, had a bit of a fight with them and stomped out. He forgot he'd left the bath running until he came back, three hours later.'

'And by then it had overflowed and soaked through your ceiling.' Gio shook his head in disgust. 'What an *idiot*.'

'I'm afraid I said something far worse than that when he came down to apologise, a few minutes ago,' she admitted. 'I would offer you a coffee, but—'

'No. It'd be dangerous to use your kettle right now,' Gio said. 'The place needs drying out, the electrics all need checking properly to make sure they're safe before you use them again, and then there's the repair to the ceiling. The carpet's probably not going to recover, so you'll need someone in to measure the room and then fit a replacement. And I'm not sure your sofa-bed is ever going to be the same again.' He surveyed the damage. 'It's going to take quite a while to sort this out. And there's no way you can stay here while your flat's in this kind of condition. Where were you planning to sleep tonight?'

She shrugged. 'I'll find a hotel or something.'

'My family would skin me for letting you do that, when I have a spare room. Problem solved—you're staying with me.' It was a rash move, he knew; after Saturday night, having Fran that close would be a major strain on his self-control. But how could he stand by and let her struggle, when such a simple solution was right at his fingertips? 'Just pack what you need for a few days. Clothes and what have you, paperwork and anything that might not cope with a high moisture content in the air.'

'Clothes?' She coughed and gestured to the rail next to the wall. The sodden canvas cover was sagging over the hangers beneath; it was a fair bet that right now the only dry clothes she owned were those she was wearing.

'OK. Have you got some large plastic bags?'

'I've got some dustbin bags.'

'They'll do. Put your clothes in those. I have a washer dryer, so we can deal with the laundry when we get back to my place.'

'We're going to carry bags of wet clothes on the Tube?'

He smiled. 'You know you say my car corners like a tank? Well, it carries like one, too. And it's parked outside. Without a permit.'

Her eyes widened. 'Gio, you'll get a fine!'

'At this time of the evening? I doubt it. And no traffic warden would be hard-hearted enough to give me a ticket when your place is flooded and your visitor permits are probably so much papier mâché.'

She clearly didn't share his certainty, but it was a risk he was prepared to take.

'Just pack your stuff and I'll carry it out for you and load it up,' he said quietly. 'Oh, and when you talk to your letting agency again, you might want to give them my home number. Just in case they need to get hold of you while you're staying with me and for some reason they can't reach you at work or on your mobile phone; the answering machine can take a message if we're not there.'

Her eyes were suspiciously glittery; she looked very close to tears. How could he stay brisk and businesslike when she so clearly needed a hug? So he wrapped his arms round her, resting his cheek against her hair for a moment. 'It's going to be all right, *piccolina*. Really.' And then he let her go before he did something really stupid, like picking her up and carrying her out to his car.

He helped her pack the rest of her clothes into dustbin liners.

'There's no point in packing these. They're dry-clean only. Ruined,' she said and made a separate pile of clothes.

Including the dress she'd worn on Saturday night, he noted. 'My mum's bound to know someone who can salvage them,' he said, picked up the pile and stowed them in a bag. 'I take it you haven't eaten yet?'

'No. I'd just done a bit of shopping on the way home.' She surveyed the squelchy mess around them. 'I don't think I'm hungry any more.'

'Fran, you need to eat properly. I know this is a horrible situation, but skipping meals will only make you feel worse.' He punched a couple of buttons on his mobile phone. 'Mum? It's Gio. I'm at Fran's—there's been a flood.'

Predictably, his mother wanted to know if he was helping Fran clear up and if she was going to stay at his flat. 'Of *course*. Look, some of her clothes are dry-clean only, and they're soaked.'

'And you need help to salvage them. Do you want me to come over to yours?'

He smiled. 'You're an angel. Yes, please. You've got my spare key.'

'I'm on my way now. Tell Fran not to worry.'

'I will.'

'Love you, Gio.'

'Love you too, Mum.' He snapped the phone closed and turned to Fran. 'Sorted. Have you called your parents yet?'

She shook her head. 'No point. They're too far away to help.'

'Don't you think they need to know where you are, in case they try to call you here and can't get through? They might be worried.'

She gave him a look as if to say, why on earth would they be worried? But she shrugged. 'I'll text them later.'

His first instinct in a crisis was to call his family. And yet Fran kept her distance from hers, sorting the problem out on her own. Was it the adoption thing that had made her so self-reliant? Or was it that she was scared to let herself be part of them, in case she was rejected again?

He remembered the way she'd suddenly tensed on Saturday night, but wouldn't tell him what was wrong. Had that been it, the idea of being part of a family and fearing rejection?

But his family had liked her immediately. They wouldn't reject her.

Neither would he.

If he could only trust himself not to let her down.

Angela and Isabella were already at Gio's flat by the time they arrived. And something smelled fantastic.

'I assume neither of you two have had the time to eat yet,' Angela said. 'So you can just sit down right now and eat.'

Fran felt the tears welling up and squeezed her eyes tightly shut. She was *not* going to be wet about this.

Angela gave her a hug. 'Hey, it's horrible when you get flooded out. Especially when you couldn't have done anything to prevent it. Sit down and eat. You'll feel a lot better when you've eaten something.'

Fran didn't quite believe her, but the gnocchi and sauce were gorgeous.

And Angela was right: it was exactly what she needed.

Fifteen minutes later the washing machine was on, Angela had made a pile of clothes she intended to take to a friend who specialised in restoring textiles, and Nonna was brewing coffee to go with the box of Amaretti biscuits she'd brought over.

'Thank you for coming to my rescue,' Fran said. 'I really appreciate it.'

'*Prego*,' Angela said with a smile. 'Of course we would. You're one of us.'

Oh, lord. She really *was* going to cry in a minute. Something inside her felt as if it had just cracked.

Gio ruffled her hair. 'Come on, *tesoro*. Let's put your things in my spare room.'

'Room' was probably a bit of an ambitious description, Fran thought; the space was more like a large broom cupboard. And it was already crammed with a computer, paperwork and three guitars. Even if he moved them all elsewhere, there wouldn't be room for anyone to sleep there.

Gio might have a spare room, but he didn't have a spare bed. She felt her cheeks scorch with heat. Was he expecting her to share his bed? And as for the message *that* would give his family...

As if he guessed what she was thinking, he said, 'I'll change the sheets for you, Fran. You'll be having my room while you stay here—and my sofa turns into a guest bed, so, before you start worrying, let me reassure you that you're not putting me out. Now, I'll show you how the shower works—there's plenty of hot water, so just help yourself whenever you want a bath or what have you. I won't be expecting you to go in to work at the same time in the morning as I do—and you don't need to come in at all tomorrow.' He took a bunch of keys from a drawer and detached one. 'Spare door key. So you don't have to wait around for me.'

She swallowed hard. 'I really appreciate this, you know.'

'Prego.' He smiled back at her.

By the time Gio had changed the bed and she'd sorted out her things in his bathroom—and it felt strangely domesticated to have her face cream sitting next to his razor on the bathroom shelf and her toothbrush next to his—Angela had finished sorting through the dry-cleaning pile. 'I'll take these to my friend tomorrow morning,' she said.

'Thank you.' Fran hugged her. 'Thank you so much. I thought they were beyond saving.'

'My pleasure, sweetheart.' Her voice softened. 'And you've already done a lot for me. If anything, I'm in your debt: Gio's not such a complete workaholic as he used to be, and he smiles a hell of a lot more.'

'Oh, Mum.' Gio groaned. 'Much more of this, and I'll be forced to put on a Derek Bailey CD.'

'Who's Derek Bailey?' Fran asked, puzzled.

'A jazz guitarist from the 1950s and 1960s. He used to do a lot of improvisation work,' Gio explained.

'It's not actually music,' Angela said, grimacing. 'It's the stuff Gio plays when he wants to clear the room.'

'Don't be such a philistine. Of course it's music. Nonna, you tell her,' Gio said.

Isabella put both hands up in a gesture of surrender, laughing. 'I'm staying out of this one.'

'It's music—but not in the traditional sense,' he said to Fran. 'It works on rhythm and texture rather than a melodic basis. What's known as tonal harmonics.'

'What's that in English? Or even Italian?' Fran asked.

In answer, Gio fetched an acoustic guitar from his spare room and demonstrated.

'See?' he said.

'Um…I'm with your mother,' Fran said. 'That's not music.'

'Why can't you play nice things?' Angela asked. 'Like the pretty bits you used to play. Like the stuff you were playing at the party.'

'And I still think you should've gone to college,' Isabella added. 'Studied music.'

Gio put his guitar away again with a scowl. 'Well, I didn't. And it's too late now.'

'Don't be silly. Of course it's not too late. There are plenty of mature students around—and you're not even thirty yet. You probably wouldn't be the oldest one there. You sort him out, Francesca,' Isabella said.

'I think,' Fran said gently, 'Gio's man enough to sort himself out.'

'Exactly. Thank you for the support, honey.' He slid his arm round her shoulders and kissed the top of her head.

Oh, lord. His closeness made her remember Saturday night. The way he'd held her and kissed her then. The way the whole room had dissolved around them. The way he'd kissed her, pressed against the front door of her flat.

'*Prego,*' she said, and hoped her voice didn't sound as wobbly to everyone else as it did to her.

* * *

Given that Gio was always in the office so early, Fran guessed that he'd go to bed reasonably early, too—so even though she wasn't tired, she feigned a yawn and said goodnight, a good hour before she'd normally go to bed.

It was weird, going to sleep in Gio's bed. Even though the sheets were clean, his scent was everywhere; and being wrapped in his duvet felt a bit like being wrapped in his arms.

Right now she could really do with a cuddle. She had no idea when her flat would be habitable again, or how much of her stuff would have to be replaced, or even if the flat would still have the same feel about it when all the repairs had been made.

'Pull yourself together. Stop being so wet. There are plenty of people in far worse situations,' she told herself fiercely. Yet still the tears slid silently down her face. She scrubbed them away and buried her face in the pillow, until at last she fell asleep.

Until a strange noise woke her.

A noise that sounded like the door opening.

For a moment, she was disorientated: then she remembered she was in Gio's bedroom. In Gio's bed. He was asleep on the sofa bed in the living room. She must have dreamed all that nonsense about the door opening. It was probably a floor-board creaking as the building settled overnight or something; and didn't people always misinterpret the noises in a strange house?

She turned over to go back to sleep.

And then she felt the mattress dip beside her.

CHAPTER TWELVE

FRAN'S first reaction was to shriek and switch on the light.

Gio also gave out the most almighty yell—and then sat bolt upright and stared at her in shock. 'Fran? What—why—how—oh, *Dio*.' He groaned and covered his face with his hands. 'I'm so sorry. When I offered you a bed for the night, I didn't mean you had to share it with me. This wasn't meant to happen. I... Look, I'm really sorry for disturbing you.' He started to slide out of the bed—and then stopped.

'Um, Fran, can you turn the light off?'

'What?'

'Turn the light off,' he repeated. 'Unless you want an eyeful. Because I'm not wearing...' He dragged in a breath and looked her straight in the eye. 'Oh, hell. This isn't what you think it is, I swear it.'

She shook her head. 'Right now, I don't have a clue what's going on.'

He swallowed hard. 'I sleepwalk. I haven't done it for years—I used to do it when I was a kid, but I thought I'd grown out of it.'

'You *sleepwalk*?' So he'd walked into her room and climbed into bed with her without realising what he was doing?

He nodded. 'Mum took me to a few doctors when I was

little. They did all kinds of tests, but it seemed there wasn't any rhyme or reason to it. Nobody knows why it happens. I just…sleepwalk.'

'And when I screamed I woke you up.' She bit her lip. 'Isn't it supposed to be dangerous to wake someone if they're sleep-walking?'

'No, that's a myth—they used to think that sleepwalkers acted out whatever they were dreaming, so if someone was dreaming about being Marie Antoinette or something and you touched them on the neck, their head would fall off. Quite how you were supposed to know exactly what they were dreaming about, I have no idea.' He smiled ruefully. 'According to re-searchers, most sleepwalkers do it in the first three hours of sleep, when your sleep's deep and dreamless. So it's not actually dangerous to wake a sleepwalker—it just throws them a bit and they might get a bit stroppy with you, so doctors recommend you just quietly guide them back to bed. If someone wakes me, I'm usually a bit disoriented and don't have a clue where I am. I certainly wasn't expecting to wake up in here.' He rubbed a hand over his face. 'I really had no idea this was going to happen, or I would've warned you. I'm so sorry I scared you.'

'You used to sleepwalk a lot?'

He nodded. 'Especially around exam times.'

'So it was stress that caused it?'

He shrugged. 'It might have been a factor, yes.'

And having an unexpected guest was definitely stressful. He'd given her his room, changed his routine for her. Which was enough, perhaps, to have made him sleepwalk tonight. Given that this was his bed, it was natural for him to return to it. 'So what exactly happens when you sleepwalk? Do you know when you're doing it?'

'No, though my eyes are open. Apparently, I used to just

walk around the house and turn all the lights on and then off again, and then take myself back to bed,' Gio said. 'Mum said they could set their watch by me. It'd be about quarter to ten when I was younger, and nearer midnight when I was in my mid-teens.'

'So that was it? You didn't used to make yourself a midnight snack or straighten pictures or anything?'

He actually blushed and looked away. 'I haven't done anything dramatic like that girl who was in the papers for climbing a crane in her sleep—or the guy who mowed his lawn in the middle of the night.'

There was a reason for the high colour in his face, she was sure. 'But?' she prompted.

'I tend to take all my clothes off first.'

'You're telling me you sleepwalk in the *nude*?' Now her initial shock of being woken had worn off, Fran could see the funny side of the situation. No wonder Gio had asked her to turn off the light. Beneath the duvet, he wasn't just bare-chested—he was stark naked.

'I was hoping for a little sympathy here.' He sounded pained. 'My sisters used to have friends over for sleepovers and they'd stay up to watch me. They knew I'd worry about sleepwalking in front of their friends, and that's exactly what used to happen.' He sighed. 'I even tried putting a lock on my door. Bolting it, too. But it didn't work—somehow I'd unlock it in my sleep and go and switch on all the lights in the house, then switch them all off again and wander back to bed.'

'Naked.' She couldn't repress a smile. 'So all these teenage girls would be getting quite a show.'

'It's not funny, Fran. Jude used to joke that she could've trebled her pocket money by making her friends pay to sleep over at our place. With me as the entertainment. And as for facing them over the breakfast table, the next morning…' He groaned. 'No way could I face a bunch of giggling teenage girls. So I used to set my alarm, go to work early with Dad and have an Italian breakfast of pastries and a latte at the café.'

She tried really, really hard to look sympathetic. But she couldn't stop the gurgle of laughter escaping. 'I'm sorry, Gio. I'm not laughing at you. It's just the thought of all these girls lining up in the playground, begging Jude to let them come and stay at your house.'

'Thanks a lot,' he said dryly. 'That really makes me feel good. Not. I thought you said you'd never laugh at me?'

When he'd told her about his first car. Impulsively, she slid her arms round him and hugged him, just as she'd hugged him that day.

But then his arms wrapped round her and the atmosphere changed.

Became charged.

'Francesca Marsden.' His voice sounded husky. Sexy as hell. 'You do realise I'm completely naked.'

'Mmm.' She couldn't quite get her mouth to move round a proper word.

'And you've just put your arms round me.'

'Uh-h-h.' Someone had glued her tongue to the roof of her mouth.

'And you're in bed with me,' he said softly. 'In *my* bed. Wearing nothing but a very skimpy nightdress.'

The v-necked top was held up by spaghetti straps. But all he had to do was push them down and the soft jersey material would fall to her waist.

She suddenly couldn't breathe.

He grazed his cheek against hers. 'This isn't supposed to

be happening.' His breath was warm against her ear, and then he was nuzzling her neck. Tiny, teasing brushes of his lips against her skin. Everywhere he touched became supersensitive; and she wanted more. So much more. She wanted him to touch her everywhere. Kiss her everywhere. Make her forget the misery of seeing the wreck of her flat.

His mouth moved down across her shoulder, nudging the strap downwards; she tipped her head back and closed her eyes as his mouth found the sensitive spot in the curve of her inner elbow.

She couldn't remember the last time she'd felt this good: but one thing she did know, she didn't want Gio to stop.

He pushed the edge of her nightdress down to bare one breast, and Fran found herself arching towards him. Wanting the touch of his hands, his mouth.

As if he could read her mind, he traced a path of kisses from her collarbone downwards; and when he drew her nipple into his mouth and sucked, she gasped, pushing her fingers into his hair to urge him on.

His tongue flicked against the hard peak, teasing her and inciting her.

And, lord, she wanted more. Wanted him to touch her much more intimately. Wanted to feel his body inside hers. 'Gio,' she breathed. 'Please.'

He stopped. 'Tell me to stop. Tell me to leave,' he said.

She opened her eyes again, but she couldn't speak.

Didn't want to speak.

'Tell me to stop, Fran. Because my self-control's starting to snap,' he warned.

She remembered the way he'd kissed her at the party. The way he'd sang to her. The way she'd wanted to be in his arms, wanted to make love with him.

And in answer she slid her hand out of his hair, hooked a finger into the other strap of her nightdress and slid it down over her shoulder so her nightdress fell to her waist.

He dragged in a breath. 'Fran, we're about to hit the point of no return. So if you want me to stop, you have to say so right now.'

She swallowed hard. 'No.'

He took her hand and pressed the tip of his tongue against the pulse that beat madly in her wrist. 'Fran, this really isn't sensible.'

She knew that. 'Right now, I don't care.' And, from the look on his face, neither did he.

'It's been driving me crazy, since I kissed you on your sofa. I've been having all sorts of fantasies about you and my desk. And then I saw you in that dress on Saturday. Kissed you against your front door.' His breath hitched. 'I wanted to carry you to bed and unwrap you. It was so hard to walk away from you that night.'

'So why did you walk away?' Not to mention staying well away from her for the last couple of days?

'Because until I find what I'm looking for, I can't make any promises.'

She was under no illusion that *she* was what he'd been looking for. Because if that were the case he would've realised by now, wouldn't he?

'And I don't want to lie to you,' he said, his voice hoarse.

She rested her palm flat against his chest, over his heart. The beat was strong and slightly fast. 'You're not lying to me. And this is as true as it gets.'

'I don't do this sort of thing.' He took her hand and pressed a kiss into it. 'I don't think you do, either.'

'No. But since Saturday night I've had this picture in my

head. Of October skies, bare trees silvered with frost under an ice-bright moon, and the heat of your body against mine.'

He hummed a few bars of the tune he'd sung to her on Saturday. 'Me, too,' he said softly. 'So let's do it. Let's have our moondance.'

Fran wasn't sure which of them moved first. Or how. Or when her nightdress disappeared—or the duvet, for that matter. But at last they were skin to skin. The contact they'd both been craving.

'You're beautiful,' she said, sliding the flat of her palm across his shoulder. Perfect muscles. Not a weak couch potato, but not a pumped-up gym freak either. Just perfect. His pecs were equally well sculpted. She loved the sprinkle of hair on his chest—just enough to be sexy—and the way it arrowed down over his abdomen. His washboard-flat abdomen. 'I'm going to paint you on the top of a latte.'

'What, and scandalise all our customers?' he teased.

In answer, she took his hand. Drew it to her mouth. Kissed the pad at the top of each finger. And then sucked the tip of his middle finger—hard.

His breath hissed. 'Fran, you've just put the most X-rated picture in my head.'

She gave him a slow, sexy smile. 'Which is exactly what you did to me when you taught me to make a latte.'

He frowned. 'How?'

'You used the word "spoon".'

His mouth curved. 'Oh, that. It's a technical term for putting froth on top of coffee. Also an item of cutlery that comes in different sizes.'

She folded her arms across her breasts. 'You're telling me you don't know another definition?'

Gently, he unfolded her arms. Bent down to drop a kiss on

each nipple. 'Oh, I do. A rather nice one. Lying curled round your body. Something like…' He shifted on to his side, moving her with him and wrapping one arm around her body to pull her back against him. 'Like this.' He splayed his hand against her ribcage. 'Almost.' He stroked the soft undercurve of her breast, then cupped her breast in his hand, rubbing his thumb over her erect nipple. 'Mmm. That's better.' His mouth grazed the curve of her shoulder. 'Is this what you had in mind?'

Her breath caught. 'Oh-h-h. Yes.'

'Interesting.' He nibbled her shoulder. 'There I was, teaching you about making coffee, and you were thinking about having sex with me.'

'I was *not*.'

'You just admitted it.'

'I was paying attention. I made notes. And might I remind you that I made you a perfect latte on your birthday? With a rosetta. Free-poured.'

'So you did.' He nuzzled the sensitive spot behind her ear. 'But you were still thinking about having sex with me.'

'May I point out that I'm not the one who invaded your bed—stark naked?'

His hand slid downwards over her abdomen. 'I can't help it if I sleepwalk. And sleepwalkers normally return to their own bed. Technically, this happens to be *my* bed.' He smoothed his hand along the curve of her hip. 'And may I point out that you're just as naked as I am?'

Skin to skin. 'So what do you have in mind?'

'Lying here with you in my arms is good.' He gently bit her earlobe. 'But I think I'd prefer it if you faced me.' He moved back slightly to give her room to turn round.

'That's better,' he said, brushing his mouth lightly against hers.

His gaze was even hotter, now.

'You have the sexiest curves I've ever seen.' He stroked the curve of her waist and hip. 'You turn me on, Fran. In a big way.' His hand drifted along her outer thigh. 'And, just so you know, I don't make a habit of this. I can't even remember the last time I dated someone, let alone anything else.' The smile vanished from his eyes. 'I might be a bit out of practice.'

'That makes two of us, then.' The same fear suddenly gripped her. 'Gio. I don't want to disappoint you.'

'You're not going to.' He held her gaze. 'Let me show you why.' His hand covered hers, warm and strong, and gently drew it down to his erect shaft. Curved her fingers round it. 'Feel what you do to me?'

It was obvious that he was in the same state as she was. So turned on that the world was spinning. She wasn't aware of anything else except Gio—the warmth and hardness of his body, the feel of his skin skating against hers, the heat in those oh-so-sexy blue eyes, the way his mouth tilted up at the ends, inviting a kiss.

An invitation she couldn't resist. She wriggled closer, caught his lower lip between hers, nipped gently until he gasped and opened his mouth and let her deepen the kiss. Let her take the lead. Kissing and touching and stroking until they were both at fever pitch.

Fran blew his mind. Simple as that. The way her fingertips skated over Gio's skin made every nerve end shimmer. And the feel of her mouth against his throat drove him crazy.

He took his time exploring her body. Stroking her skin. Kissing. Nuzzling. Nibbling. Discovering the sensitive spots that made her gasp and arch up to him when he touched her.

By the time his mouth had worked its way down to her

midriff, her breathing was shallow and her voice was husky, and she was quivering with the same intense need he felt. Because, good as this was, it wasn't enough. He needed to be inside her. Needed the ultimate closeness.

'I want you so badly, it hurts,' he whispered.

'Then make love with me, Gio,' she whispered back. 'I'm going crazy here too. I need you. Inside. Me.' A tremor ran through her body. 'Now.'

He didn't need telling twice. He rummaged in the top drawer of the little cabinet next to his bed—oh, please let that box of condoms still be there. To his relief, it was. A quick glance at the bottom reassured him they were still in date.

And then at last Fran was leaning back against a pile of pillows, her hair mussed and her lips parted and those beautiful cornflower-blue eyes all warm and inviting, and he was kneeling between her thighs. He dipped his head to kiss her as he eased into her warm, wet heat.

This was what they both wanted. Both needed.

Had he been dreaming about this when he'd been sleepwalking? Was that why he'd come here to his bed?

But it didn't matter. Because the real thing was, oh, so much better than a dream. Watching Fran's eyes widen with pleasure, feeling her breasts tightening against his chest, hearing the little breathy sighs she made as his thrusts took her higher and higher. He was aware of the pleasure rising through his own body, growing tighter and tighter. Of the softness of her skin. Of the way her body rippled round his, the tiny incoherent murmurs of pleasure she made—pleasure that echoed in his own body.

He heard her cry out his name, and then they were both falling over the edge, spinning down and down and down.

Afterwards he lay with her curled in his arms, breathing

in the sweet scent of her skin. It was the first time he'd felt at peace since the day he found his father lying senseless on the floor in the café. The black hole wasn't there any more.

Had he just found what he'd been looking for, all this time?

And, if so…how did he get to keep her?

The questions spun in his mind, but gradually he drifted into sleep. And the last thing he was aware of was the warmth of Fran's body against his. Completing him.

CHAPTER THIRTEEN

THE next morning, Fran woke to find Gio's body curled round hers, and his arm was wrapped tightly round her waist, holding her against him.

Spooned.

Muscles she'd completely forgotten about were grumbling in protest this morning. But she couldn't help smiling when she remembered last night. The promise of his kiss on Saturday night had more than been fulfilled. Incredible.

And then her smile faded. Now it was the morning. What now? Last night, they'd made no promises to each other. It had been the heat of the moment. And now...

'Good morning.' Gio pressed a kiss to the nape of her neck.

'Good morning.' Her voice sounded croaky. Nervous. Lord, this was awkward. What did she say now?

He could obviously feel the tension in her body, because he rested his cheek against hers. 'I think we need to talk, honey. Turn round and face me.'

He released his arm from round her waist; for a moment, she lay still, but then turned on her right side so she was facing him.

'So. About last night.'

Was this where he told her this was all a mistake and she'd

have to find somewhere else to stay until her flat was habitable again?

He kissed the tip of her nose. 'That wasn't supposed to happen.'

Obviously he regretted it.

He smiled. 'Though I'm glad it did.' His eyes were very blue, very honest. 'Very glad.'

So he *didn't* regret it? That was good. But... 'What happens now?'

He stroked her face. 'I don't know, Fran. I can't give you any promises.'

At least he was being straight with her.

'But I would like to find out where this takes us.' He drew her closer. 'Right now, this is just between you and me. It's nothing to do with anything or anyone else. Not my family, not the café—just us.'

The café. 'What about work?' Was she going to have to find a new job?

'Wherever this takes us, it's not going to change things at work. You're still my right-hand woman.' His lips quirked, and sheer mischief glittered in his eyes. 'Though at this precise moment you're perfectly at liberty to use your left hand on me, if you so choose.'

She placed the tip of her index finger against his collarbone, and drew a line along his sternum. 'Like this, you mean?'

He caught her hand and brought it up to his mouth. 'Oh, you tease.' He kissed her palm and folded her fingers over the kiss. 'Actually, you're right—this probably isn't a good idea.' He smiled. 'Because I'll be late for work. I need a shower. And a shave.'

She stroked his face, enjoying the faint rasp against her fingertips. 'Stubble. You look like a pirate.'

'Hmm. Which means I should carry you over my shoulder and then ravish you.' He eyed her speculatively. 'I *could* carry you to the shower…'

'And then you'd definitely be late for work.'

'Want to know something terrible?' His eyes crinkled at the corners. 'I really don't care.'

She laughed. 'Tut, tut, Gio Mazetti. If you're not careful, you'll damage your reputation as a workaholic.'

'I can think of a few people who'd kiss you for that.' His gaze was fixed on her mouth. 'I could always be their proxy.'

'So you still want to kiss me?'

His gaze grew hot. 'I want to do a lot more than kiss you, Francesca *mia*. But I have a business to run, and you need to find out what's happening with your flat.'

He brushed his mouth against hers, and it turned into a long, slow, lingering kiss that heated her blood.

'Hold that thought,' he said huskily when he broke the kiss and looked into her eyes. 'Until tonight. When I'll make it a reality.'

He vaulted out of bed, completely unselfconscious. Well, after what they'd shared, the previous night, there was no reason to be shy in front of each other. She leaned back against the pillows and grinned.

He glanced over his shoulder and raised an eyebrow. 'What?'

'Just thinking. I'd definitely pay your sister to have a sleep-over at your place and stress you into sleepwalking naked.'

He groaned. 'Oh, now that's unfair.'

'And it's a ver-r-ry nice view from here. If I were an artist, I'd definitely book you as a life model.'

He raised an eyebrow. 'Is that an offer to come and wash my back in the shower?'

She laughed. 'A moment ago, you told me to hold that thought until tonight.'

'I just changed my mind.' Before she realised what he was going to do, he walked swiftly back to the bed, scooped her up, and carried her to the bathroom.

'You're going to be late,' she warned, still laughing.

'Don't care.' His gaze smouldered as he set her back down on her feet. 'I want you. Wet and naked. And wrapped round me.'

Her heart skipped a beat at the huskiness in his tone. 'That's what I want, too.'

'Good.' He switched on the shower, stepped into the bath and took her hand. 'Come with me.' His eyes glittered. 'And I mean that in more than one sense.'

Oh-h-h. Her nipples tightened at the thought. She stopped thinking and simply stepped into the bath next to him. The water sprayed down, droplets sparkling against his skin. Wet, naked, sexy male. She couldn't resist touching him; she took the shower gel and poured it on to her palm, then started lathering his body. Starting with his shoulders, then his pecs, then down over his ribcage.

'You're playing with fire, here,' he warned.

'Actually, I'm playing with water,' she corrected, and lathered his abdomen. She watched his pupils dilate as she traced the skin on his belly, just a few millimetres away from his erect penis. Just round the outline of his erection. Not quite close enough to touch, but close enough for him to imagine and want and need.

She had every intention of driving him as crazy as he drove her.

'Francesca,' he muttered hoarsely, 'if you keep teasing me like that…'

'You'll what?' She licked her lips, enjoying his shudder of

desire in reaction. And then she poured more shower gel into her hand and slid it along his length.

'Yes.' The word was hissed between clenched teeth. 'Please. Yes. Oh.'

She loved the fact he couldn't even say the words in the right order. And she really hadn't finished yet. She sluiced the lather from him, then dropped to her knees. Bent her head. Breathed on him so he could feel the heat of her mouth, the promise of what she was about to do.

'Fran.'

It was the last coherent word he uttered. In a voice so gravelly, so out of control, that it gave her a real kick.

And then she licked him.

Teased him with her tongue.

Took him deep into her mouth, until he was quivering and tangling his fingers into her hair, urging him on.

And she loved the fact that she could make him lose control to the point where he was babbling.

'Fran.' Gio was torn between letting her take him over the edge and stopping her before it was too late.

The need to be inside her won.

Just.

Gently, he stopped her. Drew her to her feet. Kissed her hard, then lifted her so that her back was to the tiles. He slid a hand between her thighs, pushing one finger and then two inside her.

'Gio.' It was her turn to go incoherent as he found just the right spot with his thumb, circling and teasing until she was quivering, trying to buck her hips against him. Then, and only then, he cupped her buttocks with both hands, lifted her slightly, and eased his body into hers. Pushed deep. Jammed his mouth over hers to swallow her little murmurs of pleasure as his thrusts grew harder, faster, deeper.

He barely noticed that the hot water had run out; all he could think of was the way she felt around him. Like warm, wet silk. A perfect fit.

And as her body started rippling around his, tipping him into his own release, it felt like a thousand sparklers going off around them.

Gio was late for work. And when Fran finally picked up the voicemail message on her mobile phone, she only just made it back to her flat in time to meet the letting agent. Clearly he'd dealt with similar situations before, because he didn't drag out the painful part of seeing just how much damage there was; he was methodical, but thankfully he was also quick. Ceiling, floor, walls, furniture: it was just a mess.

'Keep a note of your hotel bills,' he told Fran. 'Because we'll claim those back for you.'

'I'm staying with a friend.'

'That's OK for now, but be aware that these things aren't particularly quick to sort out,' he warned. 'We have to dry the place out, repair the ceiling and then check that all the utilities work safely before you can move back in. So if you need to move to a hotel at some point, make sure you keep the bills. Now, I'm also going to need a list from you of everything that's been damaged in your personal possessions. Did you take photographs, by any chance?'

She nodded. 'That's what the London Lets office said to do when I rang last night. They're on my mobile phone.' She showed him.

'Good. Can you forward them to my email address?' He scribbled an address on the back of a business card and handed it to her. 'Or if it's easier, print them out and drop them in to the office. I'll be in touch as soon as I hear from the insurer about when we can get an industrial dehumidifier in and when we can start to replace the things you've lost.'

'Thanks.' Though even being here made Fran want to howl. It didn't feel like her home any more. Just a damp, squelchy studio flat. And even when it had dried out, she had a feeling that it would never be the same again.

It was nearly lunchtime when she walked into the café.

'Hey, we weren't expecting you today.' Sally gave her a hug and pushed a brownie into her hand. 'Gio told us what happened to your flat. Are you OK?'

'Yes,' Fran lied.

Ian handed her a mug of hot chocolate. 'You poor thing. It's a nightmare when you get flooded out. And it takes *ages* to sort out.'

She rolled her eyes. 'Tell me about it. I've spent the morning making a list of everything that was damaged. I can't believe just a bit of water can do so much damage. Or that my neighbour forgot he was running the bath and went out for three hours.'

'At least it was clean water,' Ian said feelingly. 'One of my mates got flooded out when the drains in his road couldn't cope with a downpour. Not pleasant.'

'Too much information. Especially in a café at this time of day,' Sally said, miming a 'zip lip' motion.

Ian smiled ruefully. 'Yeah. Sorry. But if I can do anything to help, Fran, just let me know.'

'Me, too,' Sally chipped in.

'Thanks, guys. I really appreciate it.' She smiled and walked into the office. Gio was sitting in her chair, making a phone call. As soon as he saw her he ended the call, swivelled round in the chair, opened his arms and tipped his head back slightly in invitation.

She couldn't resist the appeal; she leaned over and kissed him.

'No, no, you're too far away.' He pulled her onto his lap, held her close and kissed her again. 'Mmm. That's better.'

She wriggled on his lap. 'Gio, we're at work.'

He glanced at his watch. 'Officially, we're at lunch,' he corrected. There was a mischievous quirk at the corner of his mouth. 'Pity I don't have a lock on the door. Except then I might be tempted to take a very, *very* long lunch.'

'Gio. We *can't*. Not here.'

He stole another kiss. 'I'll just have to take a rain check. Until we get home.'

'Yeah. And I remember the last time you said that. "Hold that thought until later,",' she mimicked.

'Mmm.' He gave her a wide, wide smile. 'And it was worth being late for work for the first time in over ten years.'

'Ten years?' Her eyes widened. 'Gio—'

He put a finger against her lips. 'Shh. Stop worrying. Sal opened up for me and we didn't lose any customers. Though I think it's going to cost me in brownies.' He rubbed his nose against hers. 'So, how did it go this morning?'

'The flat smells to high heaven.' She swallowed hard. 'Like a dog who's been out in the rain, rolled in every puddle he can see and is just starting to dry off.'

He grimaced in sympathy. 'Ouch. Unpleasant.'

'But the agency was really good. They're putting the wheels in motion, getting the insurance company to bring in an industrial dehumidifier to dry the place out.' She sighed. 'The carpet's shrunk already, so I think they're just going to rip it out.'

He stroked her hair. 'You OK?'

'Yes. Well, no,' she admitted, and leaned her head against his shoulder. 'It didn't feel like my flat any more.'

'It will do. When it's dried out, the ceiling's fixed, there's a new carpet and we've painted the walls. It'll be fine.'

She damped down the surge of disappointment. Honestly, how ridiculous could she get? Of *course* she was going back to her own place when it was habitable again. Moving in with him was only temporary; and, had he not sleepwalked the previous night, they wouldn't have shared a bed either.

'But until then,' he said softly, 'I hope you stay with me. And I know I'm being selfish, but I hope they take absolutely ages to fix everything.'

Oh-h-h. If he'd asked her to walk to the moon and back for him, right at that moment, she would've said yes.

'Thank you.' And please don't let him notice that her voice had just gone all croaky.

He kissed the hollow of her collarbones. 'What do you want for dinner tonight? I'll cook.'

She strove for a light, teasing note. 'If you work as late as you usually do, that means we'll be eating at midnight.'

'I'll come home early.'

'Early as in a normal person's "early"?' she tested.

He laughed. 'Probably not.'

'How about I cook for us, then? If you trust me in your kitchen.'

'Of course I trust you.' His smile turned wolfish. 'But there's a condition attached. I get to sleep with the chef tonight.'

'Sleep?'

He nibbled her earlobe. *'Eventually,'* he whispered, sending a thrill of pure lust down her spine.

'Giovanni Mazetti, just how am I supposed to get any work done when you put thoughts like that into my head?'

'You're not.' He brushed his mouth against hers. 'You're going out to lunch with me. And then you're going to play hookey.'

'With you?'

He smiled. 'I'm tempted. Seriously tempted. But, no, what I had in mind is going for a spa afternoon. The sort of thing my sisters do when they've had a rough week.'

'A spa afternoon.'

'Massage, facial, something like that. Bella swears by it. It'll de-stress you.'

She shook her head. 'I'm fine.'

'No, you're not.' He held her just a little bit closer. 'Maybe I'll give you that massage myself, then. I told you to take today off, and I meant it. Go and do something to relax you. Rent some DVDs and spend the afternoon watching films, or what have you. And that,' he added, 'is an order.'

'Maybe.'

But when they'd had lunch out—a bacon, mozzarella and avocado salad in a little restaurant on the South Bank—and Gio had gone back to work, Fran decided to take his advice to do something to relax her. A wander through Kew Gardens went a long way to restoring her equilibrium. Then she went back to Gio's flat via the supermarket, texted him to remind him that she was cooking dinner and it would be ready at half past seven, and enjoyed herself cooking in a decent-sized kitchen for once.

'I might have to change your job,' Gio said when he walked in at quarter past seven. 'Forget being my office manager. You can be my personal chef instead.'

She raised an eyebrow. 'That's a bit rash. You haven't tasted dinner yet.'

'It smells fabulous, so it'll be gorgeous.' He stood behind her and slid one arm round her waist, pulling her back against him. 'And so are you.'

'Behave,' she admonished, though she was smiling.

'Oh, yeah. That reminds me. These are for you.' He brought his other hand round, and gave her a bunch of bright pink gerberas.

He'd bought her flowers. Again. Completely unexpectedly. Her throat closed and she had to blink back the tears. 'Thank you. They're beautiful.'

'Do I get a kiss, then?'

She smiled. 'After you've eaten. I need to put these in water.'

'Ah. There might be a problem.'

'What?'

'I don't actually own a vase.' He rummaged in the kitchen cupboards and came up with a couple of pint glasses. 'That'll teach me to make a romantic gesture without thinking it through first.'

She put the flowers into water and stood them in the middle of the table, then slid her arms round his neck and kissed him lightly. 'Thank you, Gio. The vase doesn't matter. It's…'

'Hey. They were meant to make you smile, not cry.' Gently, he brushed away the single tear with the pad of his thumb.

'I'm being wet.'

'No. You've just seen your personal space ruined. And you've been putting a brave face on it.' He hugged her. 'Everything will be fine. I promise.'

She swallowed hard. 'Go and sit down. I'll serve dinner.'

By the time she'd put the bowl of salad on the table and

spooned the chicken arrabbiata over the pasta, she'd managed to choke back the tears again.

'I'm not sure if I dared cook pasta for an Italian,' she said, placing the plate in front of him.

He laughed. 'You can't exactly ruin pasta.'

'Yes, you can. You can overcook it so it's soggy. Or not drain it properly.'

He took a mouthful. 'This,' he said, 'is textbook *al dente*—absolutely perfect—and that arrabbiata sauce has one hell of a kick.'

'Too hot?'

'Nope. Just perfect. And the wine's good, too. Barolo, yes?'

Trust him to know. She smiled. 'Of course. I can just imagine your face if I'd served you French wine.'

He laughed. 'My favourite wine's French, actually. Margaux. It tastes of vanilla and blackcurrant. Oh, and talking of tasting—want to come with me to a cupping? I normally go with Dad, but he asked me if you'd join us next time. I think he's planning to teach you some of the stuff he's taught me.' He grimaced. 'Sorry. My family really takes over.'

'No, I'd love to.' And it still stunned her how quickly the Mazettis had taken her to their hearts. Made her feel part of them. Her phone had been beeping all day with texts from them. From his sisters, suggesting a night out to see a really girly film with lots of popcorn to cheer her up—and Marcie had also offered to go with her when she needed to buy new furniture. From Angela, saying that her friend could repair all the damage to Fran's clothes. From Nonna, just sending her a hug.

She *belonged*.

Much more than she did in her own family. Here, she fitted in.

After dinner, they washed up together. Something she wasn't used to, and it felt weirdly domesticated. Even more shockingly, she realised that she actually liked it. The whole domestic routine.

Which Gio definitely didn't want.

She was going to have to be really careful here. Gio wasn't offering her for ever. 'For now' was as good as it was going to get. And if she let herself fall too deeply for Gio and the warm, noisy, loving family that came with him as a package deal, she was going to end up with a broken heart.

She needed to keep a distance between them, however small.

'You've gone quiet on me. What are you thinking?' Gio asked.

She shook her head. 'Nothing important.' Nothing she'd admit to. 'Would you play your guitar for me again?'

He leaned against the worktop and stared at her. 'Are you in a conspiracy with Nonna and my mum to make me go to college?'

'No. I just like it when you play.' She smiled. 'As long as it's something pretty and not that tonal harmonics stuff.'

He laughed, but fetched one of the guitars from his spare room, perched on the arm of the sofa and played Mozart to her. She watched him, taking in every detail. How his beautiful hands moved. The passion in his face as the music took over— so similar to the expression on his face when he made love.

Then he looked up, gave her a slow, sweet smile, and played a tune she recognised: an arrangement of 'I Can't Help Falling in Love with You'.

Was he trying to tell her something?

Her heart missed a beat. No, of course not. And she had to remember not to fall for him. Though the song was way,

way too appropriate. 'So you're turning into Elvis now?' she said lightly.

He smiled. 'Hardly. And, for your information, two of the three composers of that song were Italian.'

'Yeah?'

'Yeah.' He played it again, but this time instead of picking out the melody he strummed chords and sang it to her.

Lord, he had a gorgeous voice. A voice that made her melt.

'The simplest tunes are the best ones,' he said when he'd finished, and replaced the guitar in its case. 'So. I've played for you.'

'Sung for your supper.'

He lifted his forefinger. 'Ah, but all good musicians expect payment as well as supper.' He paused. 'A kiss will do.'

'A kiss.' She stood up, reached up to him and brushed her mouth against his.

'Call that a kiss?' Gio tipped her back on to the sofa and gave her a wicked smile. 'Let me show you how it's done…'

CHAPTER FOURTEEN

THE next two weeks were the happiest Fran had ever known. Her days were spent in a job she loved, and her nights in Gio's arms. He taught her about every erogenous zone in her body, including some she hadn't even known existed; the way she responded to his touch scared her, because she'd never felt anything this intense before.

And then Gio really shocked her.

'You're going to be late for work,' she said—her body clock now used to the time he got up to leave for the coffee shop.

'Nope.' He smiled at her. 'Not today.'

She frowned. 'You're in late?'

'Day off.'

She blinked. 'Run that one by me again.'

He laughed. 'You heard.'

'Are you ill?'

He rolled his eyes. 'I just have plans.'

She tried to douse the spark of disappointment that those plans obviously didn't include her. Of course he needed her to be there in the office. That was her job. Running the café chain when he wasn't around.

He didn't offer to meet her for lunch, either. But she shoved it out of her mind and just got on with work, staying late to help Sally lock up the Charlotte Street café.

When she opened his front door she discovered what Gio's mysterious plans were. Something smelled fantastic, and explained the little bistro table in the living-room alcove set with a white damask table cloth and proper silver; there were scented tea-light candles in the middle of the table and the tablecloth was scattered with rose petals.

Gio came to stand behind her and wrapped his arms round her, resting his cheek against hers. 'Good day?'

She nodded. 'And everything's ticking over fine, so you don't need to worry about anything.' She indicated the table. 'You've gone to a lot of trouble.'

'Well, you've done nearly all the cooking while you've been staying here. I thought it was time to even up the balance a little.' He nuzzled the curve of her neck. 'Go and sit on the sofa. I'll bring you a glass of wine.'

Perfectly chilled pinot grigio. Then he fetched one of his guitars and played her some of the pretty Italian divertimenti he knew she liked.

'I feel thoroughly spoiled,' she said with a smile.

And the food was even better. Grilled scamorza, followed by grilled salmon on a bed of garlicky spinach with polenta, and then the most fantastic white chocolate cheesecake.

'This,' Fran said, 'is to die for.'

'I had a rather more, um, *interesting* reward in mind,' Gio said. She grinned. 'Oh, really?'

'Uh-huh. Food of love. I've played to you, I've fed you, we're going to ignore the washing up, and you're going to have to wait for your coffee.' He took her hand and tugged her to her feet, then drew her into the bedroom.

Fran's eyes widened when she saw the rose petals scattered on the bed.

'I told you I had plans,' Gio said, sliding his fingertips under the hem of her top and drawing tiny circles against her skin.

It took him a long, long time to undress her. Every inch of skin he uncovered had to be stroked. Kissed. Licked. And by the time he finally laid her down on his bed of rose petals, Fran was shivering.

'Now. Please, now,' she whispered. Begged. She needed him inside her—right here, right now.

Gio shook his head. 'Tonight,' he told her, his eyes a sultry deep blue, 'we're taking it slowly.'

So slowly that she thought she was going to go crazy. Time and again, Gio brought her just to the edge of climax— then paused for just long enough to keep her on the brink. Her whole body had turned into a mass of sensation, aware of his tiniest movement.

And when he finally entered her—still keeping the pace slow and measured—she came instantly.

'I haven't finished yet,' he whispered in her ear. 'And neither have you.'

She didn't believe him. But when the aftershocks had died away, he began to move again. Stoking her pleasure higher and higher.

'This—' She shook her head. 'I can't…I've never come twice. It's not poss… Oh-h-h.'

He brushed his mouth against hers. 'Something you should know, *tesoro*. I'm aiming for three.'

* * *

Fran's look of shock mingled with disbelief and sheer pleasure gave Gio a real kick. He'd thought it would be good between them, but this was something else. He loved the way she responded to him. The way her body was so in tune with his. The flare of passion in her eyes. The scent of the roses mingled with the musky scent of her arousal. The sound of her little sighs of pleasure. And when his own climax rippled through him, he felt Fran's body quiver in answer. Each beat of her heart matched his own. Two as one.

He wasn't ready to say the words.

But he hoped to hell she knew exactly what his body was telling her.

And that she felt the same way.

'Can I speak to Fran Marsden, please?' the breezy voice asked when Gio answered the phone.

'Sorry, she's not available at the moment.' Jude had annexed her for lunch. Which was how come Gio was left with a panini, a chocolate brownie and a sense of disappointment. Weird how he'd got used to actually taking a proper break. Going for a stroll with Fran in Regent's Park at lunchtime and enjoying the sunshine he hadn't really noticed in years; sitting by the lake, watching the swans and the squirrels with his arm round his girl. Perfect.

'Can I help?' he asked.

'It's London Lets. Can you tell her that the flat's finished? The repairs have been done and checked, the utilities have all been tested, there's a new carpet down and she can move back in again whenever she likes.'

So soon? He carefully schooled his voice to neutral. 'Sure. I'll tell her. Thanks for calling.'

But when he replaced the receiver he sat for a while with his elbows propped against his desk and his chin resting on his hands, staring into space.

Fran could move back home again.

Out of his flat.

He didn't actually *have* to tell her about the call. He could just 'forget'. But she'd find out anyway because the letting agency was bound to ring again to see when she was planning to move back in.

Part of him wanted to give her the message—and then ask her not to go. To stay with him, to move in to his flat properly.

The more sensible part of him knew it was a bad idea. For a start, he didn't know if she'd say yes: Fran had already made it clear that she liked having her own space, and she took up so little room in his flat that you'd hardly know she was staying. Even in the bathroom, her things were kept neatly and separately from his, and could be packed in about three seconds.

But even if she did say yes…he still wasn't sure. Was he simply trying to fit into the role his family wanted for him, settling down at last? Or did he want Fran for himself? And was he the right one for her in any case? Would he end up letting her down, the way he'd screwed up with his family all those years ago?

He didn't have the answers. Needed time to work it out.

Which meant letting her go back to her own place.

And didn't they say that if you wanted someone to stay, you had to give them the freedom to go?

Lord, he hoped she'd decide to stay.

When Fran returned from lunch with Jude, full of smiles and laughter, he couldn't bring himself to tell her the news straight away. It took him an hour to work up to it. And then, keeping his voice light, he said, 'Sorry, I meant to tell you. The letting agency rang while you were at lunch. Your flat's ready.'

'Right.' Her expression went straight into neutral. Which meant he hadn't a clue what was going on in her head. Couldn't read a single signal.

'So I wondered if you wanted a hand. Maybe paint the place the colour you like, before you move back in.' In other words, stay with him a bit longer.

'I... Thanks. That'd be nice.'

He wasn't sure if her smile reached her eyes, because she'd turned away.

'I need to get a new sofa bed, too. And shelving. And curtains.' She shrugged. 'Though the colour's going to depend on what colour carpet they've put in. Something neutral, I hope.'

'Why don't you take the rest of the afternoon off and go have a look?' he suggested. 'You've put in more than enough hours lately to make up the time. And it'd be better to see it in daylight than evening light.'

'Yeah, you're right.' She nodded. 'Thanks.'

He smiled. 'I'll see you later.'

'Sure.'

Though he noticed she didn't kiss him goodbye.

He really, really hoped that wasn't a bad sign. But he had a nasty feeling that everything was unravelling around them.

Well, what did you expect? Fran asked herself as she got on to the Tube. That he'd ask you not to go—that he'd suggest moving in with him properly?

How stupid could she get?

Number one, this had all started off as a fake relationship, to keep his family happy.

Number two, what had happened between them since her flat had been flooded—well, despite that amazing night where he'd cooked for her and made love with her in a bed of rose petals, to the point where she'd felt as if their souls had connected, it was still early days. And the fact that Gio was prepared to let her go so easily showed that he wasn't ready to make their relationship a real one.

He might *never* be ready.

It wasn't necessarily her—if she thought about it rationally, she knew Gio probably wouldn't be ready to commit to anyone for a long, long time, because nothing was going to tame his restlessness—but it still hurt. And it was very clear to her now that once she'd moved back to her own flat and Isabella had returned to Milan, later in the week, they'd be reverting to their original plan.

Ending the 'relationship' quietly.

She knew now that she couldn't face working with him afterwards. Not as his 'ex'. Having to deal with the disappointment of his family and the sympathy of their colleagues would be way too messy. And the idea of watching from the sidelines when Gio was ready to let himself fall in love—with someone else...

It left her no choice.

Quite how she was going to get through Isabella's farewell dinner, she had no idea. But she was going to act as if her life depended on it. No way was she going to let Gio see how much this hurt.

When she got off the Tube again, she called the letting

agency. Yes, the insurance was paying up; they had her claim in progress; and the money should be with her next week.

Which meant she could go and buy new furniture now. On her credit card. Because by the time the bill came in the insurance money would be there. And even if it was late that wasn't a big deal, because she still had her redundancy money in a high-interest account.

Organising was what she did. Really, really well. And keeping busy was a good way of not letting herself think about the way her personal life had just disintegrated. Even so, by the time she reached her flat, Fran was thoroughly dejected. She unlocked the door and took a cursory look around.

Home.

It didn't feel like home. Wasn't her space any more. It was just a very small studio flat. The walls were magnolia, perfectly liveable with. The carpet was beige. Also liveable with. And the neutral décor meant it wouldn't matter what colour she chose for her furniture.

She didn't actually care what colour the furniture was. As long as it was delivered quickly. And there was one way to make very sure that happened. She went to one of the furniture showrooms that let you take things away there and then instead of waiting six to eight weeks for it to be made and delivered. Bought curtains and cushions, chose a sofa bed and shelving and talked the store into delivering it all the following morning.

And one night sleeping on the floor wasn't going to hurt her, was it?

She went back to Gio's flat and packed her things. Called a taxi. And was in the process of writing him a note to explain where she'd gone when the front door opened.

* * *

'Fran?' Gio stared at the suitcases next to her. 'What are you doing?'

'Moving my stuff back home,' Fran said simply.

She was leaving already? But... 'Hang on, don't you need to sort out some furniture first?'

'Done.'

That was the problem when someone was as efficient as Fran. They could sort things out at the speed of light. Anyone else would've had to wait at least six weeks for the furniture to be delivered. Not her. 'What about paint? I was going to help you paint the walls.' It would take at least a day to do that, and they'd need another day to air the place to get rid of paint fumes. That would give him two days—with any luck, enough time to work out how to get her to stay.

'Paint's not a problem. I can live with magnolia walls.'

So he didn't even get the two days he'd been banking on? Oh, hell.

He stared at the suitcases in dismay. 'You're going *now*? Right this very minute?' She'd been planning to leave without saying goodbye to him?

'You've been very sweet to put me up while my flat's been uninhabitable. But everything's fine now. So it's not really fair to put you out any longer.'

She hadn't put him out. Far from it. She'd turned his flat into his home instead of just a place to sleep and maybe eat. 'Fran—'

But what he'd intended to say was cut off by a beep from outside.

'That'll be my taxi,' she said.

He really didn't want her to go.

But she clearly couldn't wait to leave, or else she wouldn't have packed so fast, would she? So although he'd thought that the last couple of weeks had changed everything between them, maybe it hadn't been the same for her.

She was leaving.

And their relationship was back to being a fake. Something to stop other people being hurt.

He hadn't bargained on getting hurt, himself.

And he didn't know if he could go through with this. Pretend in front of his family that everything was fine, when it was very far from fine. He raked a hand through his hair. 'Look, do you want me to make some excuse for you at Nonna's dinner on Thursday?'

She shook her head. 'No, I'll be there. I want to be able to say goodbye.'

Another blast of the taxi's horn. The kind of length that meant, *I do have other fares to pick up, you know, so will you stop messing about and hurry up?*

'I'd better go,' she said, picking up her suitcases. 'Apologies for the short notice, but I'll need to take tomorrow morning off. I'm expecting some deliveries. But I'll work late to make up the time.'

'Whatever.' He was too numb to protest.

'Thanks for everything, Gio.' She picked up her suitcases. 'I'll see you later.'

'Let me take those.' He didn't want her to go—but he wasn't going to stand by and watch her struggle. His hand touched hers as he took the cases from her, and the contact made his heart contract sharply.

This couldn't be happening.

Shouldn't be happening.

If she hugged him goodbye, that would be it. He was carrying her back to his flat and to hell with the taxi driver.

But she didn't. She just gave him a really, really bright smile—as if she were truly delighted to be going back to her own space. 'Thanks for everything, Gio.'

The door closed.

And the taxi drove off.

Gio walked up the stairs to his flat. And even though there wasn't actually that much missing—Fran, being neat and tidy, hadn't taken up much room in the first place—the place seemed empty. Echoey.

The whole heart of it had gone. With Fran.

He couldn't settle to anything that evening. Although he went through the motions of cooking a meal, dinner for one felt completely wrong. Like a discord. In the end, he stopped toying with his food and scraped it into the bin. Music didn't make him feel any better, because he kept thinking of the times he'd played to Fran, the light in her eyes. And there was nothing on television.

He couldn't face going to bed. It was too big, too wide, too empty without Fran in his arms. So he sat on the sofa, flicking channels aimlessly and just wishing. Wishing that he'd never been stupid enough to let her go.

Not home. Not even a flat. After the space she'd shared at Gio's, it felt more like a broom cupboard. Not *her* broom cupboard, either. Fran hadn't yet replaced her ruined books, and although she'd managed to salvage her photographs there wasn't anything to stand them on. So she hadn't unpacked them and the place felt as impersonal as a hotel room.

Her wardrobe rail had dried out, so she mechanically replaced her clothes on the hangers. She had to clench her jaw hard when she unpacked the party dress—the dress she'd been wearing when Gio had first kissed her properly, when he'd sung for her. The dress she'd thought was ruined, but Angela's friend had salvaged. It would definitely have to go to a charity shop. She couldn't handle the memories.

So much for thinking what they'd shared was special. He'd hardly been able to wait to get his space back. He'd even offered to help her paint the walls, he'd been that keen for her to go.

She dragged in a breath. Her world had collapsed before. This time it was going to be a hell of a lot harder to build it all back up again.

But she'd do it. She'd get there. And never, ever again would she lose her heart to someone.

Even turning the shower thermostat to near-on freezing didn't make Gio feel any more awake the next morning. He'd slept so badly that he felt hungover—as if he'd drunk way too much cheap red wine. Paracetamol went a little way to muffling the pain in his head, but he felt lousy.

Today, he'd talk to Fran. Tell her how he felt. Lay his heart on the line and ask her to move back in with him.

But Fran walked into the office dead on nine o'clock, all bright-eyed and bushy-tailed, as if everything was perfectly all right with her world. 'Good morning.'

And the words Gio had planned to say stuck in his throat. She was obviously quite happy with the situation. Pleased to be back in her own space. So if he asked her to move back in with him, it was obvious that she'd say no.

'Morning,' he muttered.

If she noticed he looked like hell, she didn't comment. Simply slid into her seat and started working through the morning's post.

And Gio's world turned just that little bit darker.

How the hell could he stay with her in the office? No way was he going to be able to get any work done. His concentration was shot to pieces. All he wanted to do was wrap his arms round her and kiss her stupid. And she was acting as if nothing had ever happened between them—that they'd only ever had a business relationship.

He couldn't handle this.

'Gotta go to Docklands,' he muttered, and left. Before he did something stupid.

Like beg.

CHAPTER FIFTEEN

GOING to Isabella's farewell party at Netti's restaurant was the hardest thing Fran had ever had to do. To walk in, greet the Mazettis and chat with them as if nothing was wrong, when she and Gio had barely spoken to each other all week and things were decidedly awkward between them.

She knew he found the situation as difficult as she did, because he'd avoided her. There had always been a meeting he'd needed to go to. Or a problem at one of the branches he needed to sort out. Or something to do with the franchise. He hadn't even picked up the phone to talk to her; he'd sent her text messages or emails instead. They'd agreed by voicemail that they'd arrive separately at the party; their cover story was that he'd be 'late' because she hadn't been able to get him out of the office.

And now they had to pretend, for Nonna's sake, that everything was perfectly fine.

Thank goodness everyone kept swapping seats between courses so she didn't have to sit next to Gio. If he'd draped his arm round her shoulders or picked her up and shared her chair—as he'd been doing for the previous few weeks—she wouldn't have been able to resist nestling closer to him.

Which, considering that he'd made it very clear he didn't want to take their relationship further, was completely pathetic.

And Fran wasn't going to let herself be pathetic.

She was just really, really glad she'd dressed up tonight. Posh underwear to make herself feel special, high heels to boost her confidence, and full make-up with a concealer to hide the dark shadows under her eyes.

Tonight she was going to smile and smile and smile.

To hide the fact that her heart was breaking.

How could Fran do this? Gio wondered. How could she sit and chat so easily to his parents and his sisters and his grandmother and his cousins, as if nothing was wrong? How could she laugh at Ric's terrible puns and make a fuss of the kids and filch the last one of Netti's cheese discs from the plate in the centre of the table and just be so damned *normal*?

He was finding it a hell of a struggle.

And then it got worse.

'Gio. You've been sitting too far away—because, as always, you were late to dinner,' Isabella said, tutting. 'Come and talk to me.'

There wasn't a spare seat next to his grandmother. Because Fran was sitting there.

Hell, hell, hell.

His family was used to him scooping Fran up and sitting her on his lap. He'd done it ever since that first Sunday lunch at his parents' house. So he knew they'd expect him to do it now. If he didn't, they'd guess that something was wrong between them. But if he did…would Fran mind?

Then again, she was playing along tonight. Pretending everything was normal, for Nonna's sake.

And playing along with his family's expectations meant that he could hold her again.

It was too much for him to resist. So he walked over with

a smile, scooped Fran out of her chair and sat in her place, settling her on his lap.

He could feel the warmth of her body through the little black dress she was wearing. And he could also feel the tension running through her; her body was almost rigid. As though she'd snap if either of them moved.

Clearly she *minded*. A lot.

But he couldn't see a way out of this without giving some very awkward explanations he'd rather not make. So he simply smiled and chatted to his grandmother as if he didn't have a care in the world—and hoped that nobody in his family was trying to read his body language. Or Fran's.

This was unbearable, Fran thought. Gio had been keeping his distance, and she could cope with that. But now they were up close and personal, sitting on his lap as if they couldn't bear to be any further apart…

Oh, lord. Her body remembered just how his skin felt against hers. Just how his body felt inside hers.

And how she wanted him to touch her. Cover every inch of skin with kisses. Tease her until she was on the knife-edge of climax—and then take her over with him, all the way.

She shivered.

'Are you all right, Fran?' Ric asked. 'You look a bit…'

She felt Gio tense.

Well, she wasn't going to blow their cover at this late stage. Not after all the work they'd put into it. 'A bit sad,' she said. 'Yes, I am. Because Nonna's going back to Milan when I'm only just getting to know her, and it'll be too long before she's back here again.'

Right answer. She felt Gio relax again.

Though his arms were still wrapped round her waist,

holding her close to him. Too close for comfort, and not close enough to satisfy the ripples of desire running down her spine.

But she wasn't going to beg.

He'd made his position clear.

And she'd respect that.

'I'm coming back at Christmas,' Isabella said with a smile, 'though you can always come to Milan. In fact, yes. Gio, you should bring Francesca over to see the rest of the family. And no excuses about being too busy at work. It's time you had a holiday, too.'

'Sure, Nonna. We'll work something out,' he said.

At long, long last the party was over. And Fran couldn't stop herself hugging everyone extra hard at the end of the evening. Because this was going to be the last time she saw them. This wasn't goodnight. Wasn't *ciao*. It was *arrivederci*—a formal and permanent goodbye.

She'd loved having a family to belong to. A family where she fitted in instead of feeling stranded on the edges.

As for Gio—she didn't dare think about what she felt for Gio. Because she knew she'd crumble, right here, right now. At least she'd had the foresight to call a taxi, so she didn't have to deal with the awkward situation of Gio feeling obliged to take her home.

Fran slept badly that night.

By the morning she'd made her decision. This really couldn't go on; there was only one solution. One that was going to hurt like hell—but it was better than letting everything drag on, never letting the scars have a chance to heal.

To her relief, Gio was actually in the office when she walked in.

She closed the door behind her and leaned against it. 'Gio.'

He swivelled round in his chair. 'What?'

'I'm sorry. I can't do this,' she said. Her throat felt as if it were filled with sand. Choking.

She was *not* going to break down and cry. She was going to do this with dignity.

'I know we said a week's notice on either side, but it's not a good idea. I'll forfeit a week's wages in lieu of notice.' Money wasn't the most important thing here. She had her redundancy pay and her 'garden leave' from the studio. But she needed to leave now. Before she made a complete and utter fool of herself.

She was leaving?

Leaving Giovanni's?

For good?

Gio stared at her, so shocked he wasn't capable of uttering a single word.

'Sorry to let you down. I hope the franchise thing works out okay for you. Um, bye.'

And that was it.

The door closed behind her again.

She was gone.

It hurt. It felt as if her heart were being torn out with a rusty spoon to walk away from Gio, to walk away from the colleagues she'd become fond of and the family she'd felt part of.

But Fran knew without a doubt it was the right thing to do.

Because Gio hadn't even tried to stop her.

Quite what she was going to do now, she wasn't sure. But she was going to walk out of the coffee shop with her head held high. And nobody was going to see her tears.

* * *

The black hole was back.

Except it was bigger than before.

A lot bigger, Gio thought savagely.

And throwing himself into work didn't help. At all. Without his perfect office manager to be part of it, the franchise scheme had lost its appeal. He couldn't care less any more about corporate identities and how to blend it with regional specialities.

Without Fran, nothing mattered.

Even his old stress relief—playing technically difficult pieces on the guitar—didn't help any more. Because he kept remembering the nights he'd played to her, sung to her. The time he'd sung for his supper—and she'd rewarded him with kisses. Kisses that were gone for good.

He was sitting in his office after a week in hell, staring into space, when he heard the door close.

Fran?

No, of course not. He pushed the hope down before it had time to grow. He spun round in his chair to see his mother standing there, and pinned a fake smile on his face. 'Hi, Mum. How's it going?'

'That's the question I want to ask you,' Angela said.

'Fine, fine.' He flapped a hand dismissively. 'Just a bit busy with the franchise stuff.'

'Which is why you haven't called home for a week. Why you've ignored every single text from your sisters and you don't answer your mobile phone. Why you take your office phone off the hook every evening and stay here until stupid o'clock. And why you never return any messages from your voicemail or answering machine.'

Gio forced his smile to widen. 'I'm fine, Mum. Just busy.'

'Right.' She walked over to him and traced the shadows under his eyes with the tip of her finger. 'So that's why you have these, is it? And you've lost weight.' Her mouth thinned. 'You haven't been eating properly, have you?'

'Course I have,' he fibbed. Food tasted like ashes. And he couldn't remember what or when he'd last eaten. It didn't matter. He couldn't care less.

She shook her head, mouth pursed. 'Don't try to pull the wool over my eyes, Giovanni Mazetti. When you're *really* busy, you persuade Netti to do you a takeaway and you at least stop for two minutes in her kitchen for a chat. But nobody's seen you for a week.' She paused. 'Nobody's seen *Fran*, for that matter.'

Ah. He should've guessed his mother would work it out for herself.

'Are you going to tell me what happened, or do I have to nag it out of you?'

He shrugged. 'It's like you and Nonna always say. No sensible girl's going to wait around for a workaholic, is she?'

'Fran's sensible,' Angela pointed out. 'And you reformed for her. You actually started taking time out to enjoy yourself. You even took lunch breaks. And yet the day after Nonna went back to Milan, you broke up with her.' She shook her head. 'Something doesn't quite ring true.'

He sighed. 'OK. If you want the truth, it was a set-up right from the start. I know how much Nonna wanted me to settle down. You all assumed Fran was more than just my office manager, despite the fact I told you the truth, so she agreed to be my pretend girlfriend while Nonna was in England.'

'I see.' Angela folded her arms. 'Bit of a drastic measure, don't you think?'

'Nonna sounded so happy at the idea I'd settled down.

How could I disappoint her?' He looked away. 'I've already disappointed my family enough.'

Angela took his hand and squeezed it. 'Gio, you've never been a disappointment to any of us. And if this is about when your dad was ill, that really wasn't your fault. Just for the record, he'd been having chest pains for a few weeks before the heart attack, except being your father he pretended they didn't exist and didn't tell anyone about them. And he was perfectly capable of getting a temp in to cover your shift; he didn't have to do it himself. Nobody's ever blamed you for what happened—except yourself,' she said gently. 'And nothing we could do or say would persuade you of the truth. It drives me crazy that you're still wearing a hair shirt after all these years. The business is doing so well that you can afford to take time out and do that degree in music—and you should have done it years ago. You need to do what makes you *happy*, Gio.'

Gio shook his head. 'You must be joking. Dad's nearly sixty. I don't want to give him the excuse to come back and work himself into the ground while I swan off somewhere with my guitar and indulge myself for a couple of years.'

'That isn't what I meant, and you know it. You had a good office manager. Someone who could run the whole lot while you're studying—and you'll know the business is in safe hands so you won't have to worry about it.'

Gio gestured round the office. 'The only office manager around here is me. So that isn't an option.'

'She's not working here any more, either?'

'Nope.'

She stroked his hair away from his forehead. 'Right now, you look a mess. You miss her, don't you?'

He tried to frame the lie, but he couldn't. 'Yeah,' he admitted, his voice cracking. 'I miss her like hell.'

'Because you're in love with her.'

He took a deep breath. 'It's complicated, Mum.'

'How? You love her. She loves you.' Angela spread her hands. 'What's complicated about that?'

She loves you. He'd so wanted that to be true. But it wasn't. 'She walked out on me.'

Angela frowned. 'Did you tell her how you felt about her?'

Ha. How could he?

At his silence, she sighed. 'You didn't, did you?' She rolled her eyes. 'Sometimes, I wonder how the intelligent, talented son I've always loved and been so proud of can be so *dense*. Gio, the way she looked at you gave her away. You know the reason why your little deception worked so well? Because it had all the hallmarks of truth. I could see by the way you looked at her that you were in love with her. And she most definitely felt the same about you.'

He dragged in a breath. 'Really? So why did she leave? Why did she walk out on me?'

'Because you made this hare-brained arrangement to split up with her when Nonna went back to Milan. And if you didn't tell her how you really felt about her, of *course* she'd leave. Because she's as proud and stubborn as you are and she wasn't going to stick around when she thought you didn't want her.' Angela started at him. 'I can't believe you need me to spell it out for you. Have you called her since she left?'

He gritted his teeth. 'She made it clear it was over.'

'And you're too stubborn to fight for her? Give me strength.' Angela picked up the phone and handed it to him. 'Take it from me, male pride is a very pointless thing. A very *lonely* thing. Call her. Tell her you need to talk to her. And when you see her, tell her how you feel. Be honest with her.'

Easy to say. 'What if she doesn't want me?'

'It's a risk you'll have to take. And it's about time you took it.' She dropped a kiss on his forehead. 'Call her. And then call me later and let me know how things are, OK?'

CHAPTER SIXTEEN

FRAN didn't answer her phone. Didn't call Gio back when he left a message. Ignored his texts and emails.

He considered sending her flowers; then he remembered that she was on garden leave. So she might not even be in London. She might have gone home to see her family. Then again, he knew she didn't think she fitted in with them: so it was unlikely.

So where was she? Had she gone somewhere? Taken a break to get away from everything?

There was only one way to find out. Talk to her, face to face. He went to her flat. Pressed the intercom.

No answer.

So then he pressed her neighbour's buzzer—the one who'd flooded her flat in the first place.

'If you're selling something, I'm not interested,' was the greeting through the intercom.

Charming. Gio resisted the urge to say something rude; if he put the guy's back up, he'd never get the information he wanted. 'I'm not selling something. Actually, I'm trying to get hold of your neighbour.'

'Nothing to do with me, mate.'

'I rather think it is,' Gio said, 'seeing as you flooded her flat in the first place.'

All the belligerence suddenly left the man's tone. 'Oh.'

'She was staying with—with a friend of mine. And she left some things my friend wants to return to her.'

'Well, I can take them in, if you want,' the neighbour said, his voice slightly grudging.

'No, they need to be returned personally.'

'Are you calling me a thief?'

'No, nothing like that.' Gio sighed. Poor Fran, having to put up with such an aggressive neighbour. The sort who'd fly off the handle at the least provocation. Definitely the sort who'd stomp out of his flat in a strop and forget he'd left the bath running. When Fran had had a hissy fit on him for flooding her flat, she was lucky he hadn't flattened her. 'Look, my friend hasn't been able to get in touch with her. Do you know if she's around at the moment or if she's away?'

'Her recycling box was out with the others, this morning. That's about all I can tell you.'

Not a great deal, but it was enough—it proved that she was still in London. She was clearly just avoiding all Gio's messages.

'Thanks.' He stopped leaning on the intercom.

So what did he do now? She obviously wasn't going to return his calls. If his mother was right, this was a defence mechanism to stop herself being hurt, because she thought he didn't want her. Given what he knew of her background, it was understandable she'd be wary of putting herself in a situation where she could be rejected.

But unless he could talk to her, he wasn't going to be able to tell her how he really felt about her. That he wasn't going to reject her.

Flowers weren't going to work. Or chocolates. He needed

something to show her he was absolutely serious about this. That the stakes were as high for him as they were for her.

But how?

He spent the evening brooding about it. And then he remembered her suggestion. Expanding the café chain by adding another branch would mean additional premises costs; whereas if they kept the same number of branches, but opened in the evening, the costs would all be marginal. Starting with the book group in Holborn.

So far, so sensible.

And then she'd suggesting opening the Charlotte Street café once a week.

For an evening of classical music.

With him as the performer.

Her voice echoed in his head: *play the music you love for people*.

And she'd told him to take a sabbatical. Be a musician. His old dream—the one he thought he'd stamped on and crushed years go. But the yearning was still there.

Maybe, he thought, it was time he did.

And maybe, just maybe, if he did it, it would convince her that he was serious.

Courier delivery? She hadn't ordered anything that was likely to be delivered by courier. Fran frowned, but signed the courier's form.

The envelope held no clues whatsoever to the contents. It was just a plain A5 cardboard-backed envelope. Her address was printed on a label, and the postmark was central London. Odd. At first glance, she would have said it was junk mail. But junk mail didn't usually come in a cardboard-backed envelope—and it definitely didn't come by courier.

She opened the flap, and took out the folded A4 sheet.

And blinked as she read the poster.

An evening of music at Giovanni's of Charlotte Street.

She blinked even harder as she read who was playing.

He was taking up her suggestion?

And he'd written something on one of the blank spaces on the poster. *Please come. Gio.*

His handwriting was spikier than she remembered it. As if it was an effort for him to write the note. But the words themselves were so sparse, told her nothing about how he was feeling or why he'd invited her. Was it out of some sense of obligation, because she'd been the one to suggest it? Or was it because he really wanted her there?

Just 'Gio'.

Not 'love, Gio', as his flowers had been.

Just 'Gio'. Impenetrable.

Fran thought about it. Very hard. And she didn't make her final decision until the evening of the concert.

She'd go.

But she'd slip in very quietly. Merge into the background. Once she could judge the situation, she'd know whether to go and talk to him—or whether to leave again, just as quietly.

She wasn't going to come. Gio paced his office. This was the most stupid, stupid idea he'd ever had. He should've called the whole thing off when she hadn't replied to his invitation. He knew she'd definitely received it—he'd sent it by courier so he could check whether it had been delivered and who signed for it. But she'd stayed silent.

She wasn't going to come.

And he had a café full of people out there, waiting to hear him play.

How the hell was he going to do this?

Because it wasn't his reputation on the line, at the end of the day. It was the café's. If he made a fool of himself, so be it. He could live with that. But he didn't want to undermine all the work his father had put in to Giovanni's. Or the ten years he'd dedicated to it himself.

He should have booked other acts, too. So if his own set was a complete waste of time, at least the audience would remember something good from the evening. A string quartet, a small jazz trio, a folk singer. But, no, he was doing this solo. Putting his heart and soul on the line.

And for what?

Because she wasn't going to be there.

Maybe he should've done this as a private performance. Just for Fran. And then if she hadn't turned up he wouldn't have made such a fool of himself.

Why had he been so stupid?

'Gio. You'll be fine, honey,' Angela soothed, coming in and patting his shoulder. 'This is a little bit of stage fright. Perfectly normal. Just relax.'

It wasn't stage fright. At all. 'Is she there? Could you see her?'

'You'll be fine.'

The evasion was all too obvious. She didn't want to say no because she didn't want the knowledge to hurt him. But he knew anyway, and his stomach felt hollow. Adrenalin made his fingers feel heavy and buzzy—no way could they work with the precision he needed to play Bach and Dowland and Tarrega. He was going to screw this up. Seriously screw this up.

He took a deep breath. The last night he'd played a classical concert had been the night his father almost died.

He couldn't do this.

But then his father walked in and hugged him. 'I'm so proud of you, son. Now go out there and show the world what Gio Mazetti is made of. Go and *shine*.'

'We'll be right by your side,' Angela said softly.

He couldn't let his family down. And even though he knew the one person he wanted to play for wasn't there…he'd do it.

He picked up his guitar and walked into the café. Sat down on the stool at the front of the crowd. Heard the buzz of conversation dip to a murmur and then a hush.

He wasn't going to look for Fran. There was no point. But he'd play as if she were there. Play the pretty pieces she'd loved. 'Spanish Ballad', 'Air on a G String', the 'Alhambra', Dowland…

And as the minutes ticked past, he realised.

He could still play.

He could still do this.

And he began to smile.

At last he came to the end of the set. 'Thank you for listening to me tonight,' he said. 'I'm going to play one more song for you. For someone who's very special to me. Someone I love very much, from the bottom of my heart, and I was stupid enough not to tell her so when I had the chance. She's not here tonight, but I'm going to play it for her anyway.' His voice caught. 'Because without her I wouldn't be playing here tonight. Wouldn't be playing at all.'

Tears pricked Fran's eyes. Someone he loved very much, from the bottom of his heart. Did he mean her? But she *was* here. She frowned. OK, she'd slipped quietly into the back, but surely he'd seen her?

And then he began to play. The most beautiful arrangement of a song she knew well—her parents adored musicals and her mother's favourite was *South Pacific*. 'This Nearly Was Mine' was a song that made her mother cry, about the man who was in love with a woman who didn't return his love. And this instrumental version would definitely have her mother in tears. A minute and a half of sheer wistfulness.

It practically had Fran in tears, and she could see how moved the audience was, too.

'Thank you for coming,' Gio said when the last notes died away. 'Goodnight.' And he left the café to wild applause.

Fran stayed where she was, unable to move. That song…had it been for her? A song about nearly having paradise, about the one girl he dreamed of, about kisses he remembered—did he mean her?

She dragged in a breath. Gio had played tonight. A proper classical performance, in front of an audience, for the first time in more than ten years. And he'd asked her to be here.

Maybe she was reading too much into this.

But if she didn't go to see him, here and now, she knew she'd regret it for the rest of her life.

Slowly, she made her way over to the corridor that led to the office.

Gio's parents were there. And when they saw her, Gio's father held out his arms. Hugged her.

'Go to him,' Angela said softly, and pointed to the office.

Fran nodded, swallowed hard, and opened the door.

'Hello, Gio.'

Gio's head whipped round. 'Fran? But…I thought you weren't…' His voice trailed off.

He didn't think she'd been there? 'I was there,' she confirmed. 'I saw you play. Heard you.'

'All of it?'

She nodded. 'That last song—was it for me?'

He dragged in a breath. 'Don't you know that?'

'I wouldn't be asking if I did.'

'Yes. It was.' He looked her straight in the eye. 'I played here tonight, because you suggested it. Because you're right—it's time I forgave myself and played again. Without you, I wouldn't have done this.'

'That wasn't *all* you said.'

A faint smile tugged at the corner of his mouth. 'Ah. The bit about the fact I love you from the bottom of my heart, you mean? I do.' His expression became bleak. 'And when you walked out on me…that was when I realised how stupid I'd been. That I should've told you before. Taken the risk.'

'So why did you let me leave?'

'Because you were so keen to get your own space back.'

She frowned. 'Hang on. You couldn't wait to get rid of me. You even offered to help me paint my flat.'

'Only so you'd stay with me for at least two more days—one while we painted, one for the fumes to go. Maybe one more for luck.'

'So you wanted me to stay?'

He nodded.

And now he was telling her how he felt. Taking the risk. Like he'd taken the risk tonight and played for an audience.

He'd asked her to come along.

He'd said he loved her.

Maybe it was time she took a risk, too. 'I wanted to stay.'

'So why didn't you say something?'

'Because I thought you wanted to stick to your original plan. That as soon as Nonna went back to Milan, we'd end the fake relationship.'

He shook his head. 'It wasn't a fake. It might've started

out that way—but when you stayed at my flat it most definitely *wasn't* a fake. We didn't have sex, Fran. We made love.'

'You let me go.'

'I was wrong.' He took a deep breath. 'The night of my birthday party, I told you there was a black hole inside me. Something missing. Well, now I know what fills it. What makes me complete.'

She waited.

'You,' he whispered. 'You complete me, Fran. I love you.'

'You love me.' She tested the words, almost in wonder. 'You love me.'

'You heard me say it. In front of a crowded room when I didn't even know you were there, I said I loved you from the bottom of my heart. That I was playing for you. And I'm telling you right here, right now. Francesca Marsden, I love you.'

Her breath hitched. 'I…I don't know what to say.'

'The phrase I'm listening for is "I love you, too",' he said wryly.

She did. But saying it… Lord, that was hard.

'When you walked out, I was so stunned that I couldn't even speak. And by the time I'd recovered my wits enough to call you, you'd frozen me out.' He spread his hands. 'I don't know how to prove I love you. But I do. And I know what I want from life, now. I want marriage and babies and a house full of noise and laughter and love. And,' he told her, his voice cracking, 'I want it with you.'

CHAPTER SEVENTEEN

'WAS that a proposal?' Fran asked.

'Not a proper one.' Gio spread his hands. 'I'm Italian. I want to marry you, yes—but I need to ask you the old-fashioned way.'

'The old-fashioned way? What's that?'

He smiled. 'I'm going to ask your father for your hand in marriage.'

She stared at him. 'This is the twenty-first century, Gio. People don't do that any more.'

'Yes, they do. And I want to do it the traditional way.' His gaze grew hot. 'Just for the record, I'm intending to carry you over the threshold as well. And take your wedding dress off very, very, *very* slowly.'

Oh, lord. The picture *that* conjured up. The memories of the night he'd made love with her and insisted on taking it slowly. So slowly that she'd come more than once for the very first time.

Some of her thoughts must have shown on her face, because he added with a grin, 'Spoon.'

She couldn't help laughing back. 'Behave.'

His smile faded. 'Then say the words.'

'Which words?'

'You know which ones. I need to hear them, Fran.'

Words she'd never said before.

She took a deep breath. 'I love you.'

'Didn't hear that.'

'I love you,' she said, more loudly.

'Good.' He wrapped his arms round her and kissed her. Thoroughly.

The next thing she knew, they were sitting in the office chair—and she was on his lap, with her arms round his neck.

'I missed you,' he said softly.

'I missed you too,' she admitted.

'We've been very stupid. We should've been honest with each other. Talked. Taken the risk instead of being too scared.' He brushed his mouth against hers. 'I need to see your parents.'

'No, you don't.'

He sighed. 'Fran, I shared my family with you. Why won't you share yours with me?'

'Because it's *different*.'

'Because you were adopted, you mean?' He stroked her face. 'That doesn't make any difference. They might not be your natural family, but they're still your family—they're the ones who grew up with you. And you refer to your parents as Mum and Dad, so surely you love them?'

She rested her forehead against his shoulder. 'I'm not like any of them. I'm the odd one out.'

His arms tightened round her. 'I don't think you're odd. Well, not very.' He grinned as she lifted her head. 'I thought that would make you glare at me.' His voice softened. 'Meet me halfway, Fran. At least introduce me to them. Because we're going to have a *big* wedding.'

Oh, lord. 'How big a wedding?'

'I'm part of a big family. The Mazettis are close. And even if we disappear with the intention of getting married very quietly at the top of a mountain, they'll all work out exactly where we've gone, and when we get back to base camp they'll be waiting there with a party and more confetti than you'd think could ever be made.'

From what she'd seen of a Mazetti family party, he wasn't exaggerating.

'OK. I'll call them.'

'Call them now.' He leaned forward, picked up the office phone and pushed it into her hand.

She replaced it on the desk. 'Later.'

'*Now*, Fran.'

For a moment, he thought she was going to refuse. But then she sighed, and punched in her parents' number.

'Hi, Mum. It's Fran.' She paused. 'Can I come and see you? There's someone I'd like you to meet.'

Gio couldn't catch the reply on the other end. Why hadn't he thought to switch the phone on to hands-free speaker mode?

'When do we want to come?' Fran asked. 'Um…'

He prodded her so she looked at him and mouthed, 'This Sunday.'

Fran shook her head and turned away.

He grabbed her desk pad and scribbled a note. *Ask for this Sunday or I'll ask them myself.* She'd once threatened to break the rules and look up his personal information on the staff records. He could do the same.

She scowled, but to his relief she said, 'How about this Sunday? Uh-huh. I need to check the train times, but, yes, we'll be there before lunch. OK. Bye.'

No 'I love you', he noticed. All businesslike. So very different from his own family. Well, he'd give Fran all the love she'd been waiting for. And more.

'We're not going by train,' he said when she replaced the receiver.

'Why not? Gio, my parents live in Oxford.'

'Which means it's straight down the M40. That's fine. I like driving.'

'But…'

'Not buts, Fran.' He brushed his mouth against hers. 'By the way, there are two more things you need to know.'

'What?'

'Firstly, I've just discovered I'm *very* traditional. So, much as I want to take you back to my place tonight and spend every single second making love with you, I'm not going to.' He rubbed the tip of his nose against hers. 'No sex,' he whispered, 'before marriage.'

She blinked. 'Gio, may I point out that we've already, um, done it?'

'Uh-huh.' He smiled. 'That was before you were engaged to me.'

'I'm not engaged to you. You haven't asked me to marry you.'

He waved a dismissive hand. 'That's a minor detail. I'm going to. Which makes you as good as engaged. And Italian men are ultra-traditional. No sex before marriage. Not even phone sex.'

'Phone sex?'

'Where I tell you exactly what I want to do with you. What I want you to do.' He nuzzled the sensitive spot just below her ear. 'And I'll hear the change in your breathing. Know the very second that you come—and that you're thinking of me when you do it.'

'Oh-h-h.'

He could see from her expression that the idea intrigued her. And he could feel her heat beating just that little bit faster. He licked her earlobe. 'I might just do that, some time,' he told her, his voice husky with promise. 'But not until we're married. Which leads me to number two.'

She stroked his face. 'I'm not sure I'm ready to hear this.'

'Trust me, you will be.'

'All right. The second thing?'

'Our engagement's going to be short.' He moved back slightly so he could look into her eyes, and moistened his lower lip with the tip of his tongue. 'Really, *really* short.'

'Define "short".'

He stole a kiss. 'Given that organising is your forte—how quickly can you organise a wedding?'

She laughed. 'Is that a challenge?'

'Nope. Wrong tone. I'm not challenging. I'm *begging*. And I'd prefer the answer to be something in nanoseconds.'

'A small wedding we can sort out in however long the notice period is to the register office. Days, probably. A big church wedding—well, you have banns and all sorts of things to sort out. We're talking weeks. *If* the church isn't booked up. And I'm assuming you're Catholic.' At his nod, she continued, 'I'm not. So there's all that to sort out, too.'

'How long?'

She shook her head. 'I really don't know. Can't even guess. Definitely weeks.'

He groaned and leaned his forehead against hers. 'I might have to revise number one.'

'Uh-uh.' She wagged a finger at him. 'You said you were going to do this the traditional way.'

'In which case, I'd better take you home now. And you

need to think about whether you want a big church wedding or a big register office wedding.'

'You haven't asked me yet,' she reminded him. 'And I haven't said yes yet.'

'I will,' he said. 'And so will you.' He kissed her. 'And now I'm going to take you home. Before my very poor self-control snaps. Because I remember what it feels like to be deep inside you, Francesca, and my body's screaming out to do it again.'

He gently nudged her to her feet and led her out of the office.

The café was deserted and locked up, although one bank of lights was on over the counter. Fran blinked. 'I saw your parents and your sisters earlier. I thought they'd still be here.'

Gio smiled. 'Believe me, the second I switch my phone on you'll hear beep after beep from all the text messages asking me if everything's OK and we're together again.' His smile broadened. 'For the first time ever I think they're trying to be tactful. I think they realised we needed some space.'

Her eyes glittered. 'I remember you saying once about needing a lock on your office door. Looks as if we don't need one tonight.'

He dragged in a breath. 'You've just put another of those X-rated pictures in my head.'

She gave him the sexiest smile he'd ever seen. 'Then let's make it real, honey.'

Oh-h-h. It was way too tempting. He almost picked her up in a fireman's lift to carry her back to the office and push the papers off his desk and ease into her body. But he stopped himself in time. '*Not* until we're married. But we can have dinner together tomorrow night.' He sighed. 'And I'll have to put you in a taxi at the restaurant door. On your own. Tonight as well as tomorrow.'

'You're absolutely serious about this traditional bit?'

He nodded. 'Until I've met your family and spoken to your father, I'm not going to ask you to marry me.'

She sucked in a breath. 'What if my dad says no?'

'He won't,' Gio said confidently. 'Because I'll tell him how much I love you. That I want to spend the rest of my life with you. That you're going to be my equal and I won't expect you to give up your career to have babies.' He smiled. 'Though we most definitely are going to have babies. At least one. I want a little girl who looks just like her mum, with big blue eyes I can't say no to.'

Fran gave him a truly wicked grin. 'Can't say no to, hmm?'

He kissed her. Thoroughly. And then called the local taxi firm. 'While I still can,' he said, when he'd ended the call. 'The next time we make love, it's going to be on our wedding night.'

'That,' she teased, 'is a challenge.'

'No. It's a promise.' He smiled. 'And I'll always keep my promises to you.'

CHAPTER EIGHTEEN

ON Sunday Fran was almost sick with nerves. She was awake hours before Gio was due to pick her up, and she couldn't settle to anything.

At last he buzzed through to the intercom.

'On my way down,' she said.

'Good morning, *tesoro*.' He kissed her lightly. 'All set?'

She nodded. 'I just need to get some flowers on the way.'

'Already sorted.'

Oh. Well, it would have been. Gio had impeccable manners. 'Thank you.'

She barely said a word all the way to Oxford. Gio didn't push her to talk—just occasionally reached out to squeeze her hand, letting her know that he was right beside her.

It was completely ridiculous. Of course her parents would like Gio. Everyone who met him liked him.

But—and it was a big but—she so wanted their approval. To know that she'd done something right in their eyes.

When they came off the M40, she directed him to her parents' house. As he parked in the driveway, she frowned. 'That's Suzy's car. And Ted's.'

He smiled. 'So I get to meet all of them, then? Good.'

He didn't mind?

Her thoughts must have been obvious, because he touched her cheek. 'Hey. You had to meet nearly all mine at once. There were rather more of them. And you know I want to meet your family.' He climbed out, undid her door and then collected the most beautiful bouquet from the boot of his car. Pure white roses, lilies and freesias.

Which Fran's mother most definitely appreciated, because she went pink with pleasure when Gio handed them to her. 'How lovely! Thank you.'

'My pleasure, Mrs Marsden. And thank you for allowing Francesca to bring me to lunch.'

'Do call me Carol. Please.' She smiled at him. 'Hello, Fran.'

'Hello, Mum,' Fran muttered.

This was ridiculous. She'd been an office manager for years—firstly at the voiceover studio and then for the Giovanni's chain. Competent, efficient and effective. So why did she turn into a shoe-scuffing, awkward teenager the minute she walked into her parents' house?

'I'll put the kettle on. Tea?' Carol asked.

Gio smiled. 'Thanks. That'd be lovely.'

'Warren—Fran's dad—is at the allotment, but he'll be home soon,' Carol added.

'What allotment?' Fran asked

'He's doing this stuff about eco schools, and he thought having an allotment would fit in really well with it. And he wants us to have home-grown vegetables for lunch. He's dragged the others off with him to help him cut the beans.'

Home-grown vegetables? Then Fran noticed her mother hadn't just made the usual Sunday roast. There was a chocolate cake—her favourite—cooling on a wire rack. And an apple pie ready to go into the oven when the main course was out.

'You've gone to a lot of trouble,' she said, feeling guilty.

Her mother must have spent all morning cooking. 'You didn't need to do all that.'

Carol scoffed. 'Of course I did. You're my daughter. I wanted to.'

'And I didn't think the others would be here today.'

'Dom'll probably tell you he's only here because he can't stand college food—but as soon as I mentioned you were coming today, he was straight on the phone to Ted and Suzy.' Carol smiled at her. 'They wouldn't miss you coming home, love. Though you can expect Suzy to moan about the fact she could've seen her favourite band in Manchester last night and Ted's swapped duty at the last minute to get today off.' She handed Gio and Fran a mug of tea. 'It's nice to meet you, Gio. Fran hasn't told me much about you, but then none of my four are particularly forthcoming.'

Gio smiled. 'My mother has a spy network. If we don't tell her ourselves, someone else does.'

Carol laughed. 'I'll bear that in mind.'

Just then, there was a kerfuffle; the kitchen door burst open and a young springer spaniel bounded in.

'A dog? Since when…?' Fran asked, looking at her mother.

'No, she's mine. Last week. Rescue dog,' Ted explained. 'Fran, meet Bouncer. Bouncer, this is my big sister.'

Fran could easily see how the spaniel had got her name. 'Hello.'

'Muddy paws! Oh, no. Sorry, Mum. Sorry, Fran,' Ted said, looking at the paw-prints on the floor and his sister's dress.

'Hey, mud washes out. It's not a problem.' Gio made a fuss of the spaniel. 'Hello, *bella ragazza*.' He was rewarded with a lick—and muddy paw-prints on his shirt.

'Ted's girlfriend's a police dog handler,' Suzy said. 'She's meant to be helping him train the pup. Not that it's working yet. Hi, Fran.' She gave Gio a shy look. 'And you must be Gio?'

'Pleased to meet you,' he said, shaking her hand.

Fran made quick introductions. 'And this is Dominic, and my dad,' she finished as they walked in together, laden with vegetables.

'Hello, love.' Warren smiled at her. 'I cut extra beans so you can take some home to London with you. And Dom's going to wrap some carrots up for you in newspaper—they keep better with earth on.' He looked at Gio. 'Nice to meet you, young man.'

'And you.' Gio held his hand out. 'May I have a quick word in private, Mr Marsden?'

'Warren.' He smiled. 'When Carol told me Fran was bringing you to see us, I wondered. Come into my study. Bring your tea with you.'

'Does this mean you're getting married?' Suzy asked when Gio followed their father out of the kitchen.

Fran took a sip of tea. 'Possibly.'

'Um, have you sorted out bridesmaids yet? Because if not, I'd really… Well…' Suzy wriggled on her chair. 'You know.'

Fran stared at her sister in surprise. 'You want to be my bridesmaid?'

Suzy nodded. 'I know I'm the scary dentist-to-be and all that, but—you're my big sister. And even if you want me to wear a dress that makes me look like a meringue…I won't mind.'

Carol squeezed her hand. 'And I know you're brilliant at organising, but I'd love to help you choose your dress.'

Fran really hadn't expected this reaction. Her mother and sister wanted to be involved in the wedding?

'And we'll be ushers if you want us to,' Dominic added.

'As the elder twin, I'll make sure he wears a suit,' Ted said, sitting on the floor with a wriggling puppy on his lap.

Which was when Fran realised. They were making a fuss just because she'd come home. So maybe, all these years when she'd thought she was an outsider, she'd been completely wrong. Her throat felt thick with tears and she swallowed hard. 'I'd love that. Gio…being Italian, he wants to ask Dad's permission to marry me.'

'We guessed as much. Because you never bring anyone home,' Suzy said.

'And that's why Ted—' Dominic began.

His brother nudged him hard. 'Shush, or I'll let Bouncer chew your shoes.'

'Ted *what*?' Fran asked curiously.

'Ah.' Ted stared at the floor. 'I, um, bent some rules. Looked him up on the police computer.'

Fran stared at him in shock. 'You didn't!'

He shrugged. 'Well, we just wanted to be sure he was OK. And that he treats you right.'

'He will,' Warren announced, returning to the kitchen. 'Gio and I have just had a very interesting chat.'

Fran squirmed. 'Uh-huh.'

'And I think we all need to disappear for a minute,' Warren added.

Gio shook his head. 'Absolutely not. This is the exactly the right time and the right place—in the heart of your house and the heart of your family.' He took a small box out of his pocket and dropped to one knee in front of her. 'Francesca Marsden. I have your father's permission to ask you a very important question.' He opened the box to reveal a platinum ring set with a heart-shaped diamond. 'Will you marry me?'

A heart-shaped diamond—a ring she hadn't even known

he'd bought—given in the heart of their house and the heart of her family. Fran could hardly see because her vision was blurred with tears. 'Yes,' she whispered. 'I will.'

'I think,' Warren said, 'this means champagne. So we can welcome Gio to the family properly.' It seemed to take only seconds for a bottle of champagne and seven glasses to appear. And as the cork popped, Gio held her very tightly. 'It's just the beginning,' he said softly, 'of the rest of our lives. And a very extended family.'

One that wasn't as tactile as the Mazettis and maybe didn't say it as often, Fran thought—but one that felt the same way.

With love.

EPILOGUE

Thirteen months later

'HAPPY ANNIVERSARY, Mrs Mazetti.' Gio set the tray on top of the bedside cabinet, then climbed back in bed next to Fran.

'Champagne and strawberries for breakfast?' she asked.

'It's our wedding anniversary. And I'd like to draw your attention to a very romantic gesture. There's a single red rose on that tray.'

She smiled. 'For a student, you know, that's terribly extravagant.'

He laughed, leaned back against the pillows and pulled her into his arms. 'I'm not your average student.'

'You're not average *anything*,' she murmured, kissing him.

'Why, thank you, honey.' He held her close. 'It's been quite a year. Getting married, starting up the Thursday jazz and classics nights in Charlotte Street, moving to Greenwich, opening a new branch here...' He sighed. 'Not to mention handing over a lot more of the control to the new partner in Giovanni's. Who's so damned efficient she leaves the office at five every night.'

'Something had to give. Even *you* can't do a full-time degree on top of managing a café chain,' she said. 'Especially as you have a new role to fulfil shortly.'

'Oh?' He frowned. 'What's that?'

'I have an anniversary present for you too.'

He rubbed his nose against hers. 'Mmm. I do hope it's what I think it is.'

She laughed. 'That's for later. And you're going to have to share this particular present.'

He looked at her in puzzlement. 'How? And with whom, precisely?'

'You'll see when you get the present.'

'"When" being the operative word,' he grumbled.

She sat up and opened the drawer next to her. 'Close your eyes and hold out your hand.'

He did so, and she placed a small white rectangular object on his palm.

'OK. You can open your eyes now.'

He looked at it. Stared at her. Stared back at the item on his palm. 'Fran, is this what I think it is?'

'*Sì, papà,*' she confirmed. 'You're going to have to learn to play some lullabies. Maybe compose some.'

'When?'

'About seven months.'

He whooped with joy. 'A year ago, I thought you'd made me the happiest man on earth. But today I've learned I was wrong: it's just going to get better and better. Every day, for the rest of our lives.'

Tears of sheer happiness pricked her eyes. 'I love you, Gio.'

'And I love you too, Francesca—my love, my life.' He

wriggled down the bed and dropped a kiss on her abdomen. 'And the perfect family. Where we belong.'

'The perfect family,' she echoed.

Where she most definitely belonged.

THE ROYAL HOUSE OF NIROLI

...*International affairs, seduction and passion guaranteed*

Volume 1 – July 2007
The Future King's Pregnant Mistress by Penny Jordan

Volume 2 – August 2007
Surgeon Prince, Ordinary Wife by Melanie Milburne

Volume 3 – September 2007
Bought by the Billionaire Prince by Carol Marinelli

Volume 4 – October 2007
The Tycoon's Princess Bride by Natasha Oakley

8 volumes in all to collect!